# CONTENTS

# WHITE
# STALLION
## OF LIPIZZA

By MARGUERITE HENRY
Illustrated by Wesley Dennis

ALADDIN BOOKS
Macmillan Publishing Company  •  *New York*
Maxwell Macmillan Canada  •  *Toronto*
Maxwell Macmillan International
*New York • Oxford • Singapore • Sydney*

## To Colonel Alois Podhajsky

*Director of the Spanish Court Riding School of Vienna*

whose life is dedicated to the purpose which he has expressed in his own words: "Our Spanish Court Riding School is a tiny candle in the big world. Our duty, our privilege is to keep it burning. If we can send out one beam of splendor, of glory, of elegance into this torn and troubled world, that is worth a man's life."

First Aladdin Books edition 1994
Copyright © 1964 by Rand McNally & Company

Aladdin Books
Macmillan Publishing Company
866 Third Avenue
New York, NY 10022

Maxwell Macmillan Canada, Inc.
1200 Eglinton Avenue East
Suite 200
Don Mills, Ontario M3C 3N1

Macmillan Publishing Company is part of the Maxwell Communication Group of Companies.
Printed in the United States of America
10  9  8  7  6  5  4  3  2  1
A hardcover edition of *The White Stallion of Lipizza* is available from Macmillan Publishing Company.

Library of Congress Cataloging-in-Publication Data
Henry, Marguerite, date.
White stallion of Lipizza / by Marguerite Henry ; illustrated by Wesley Dennis.—1st Aladdin Books ed.
p.    cm.
Summary: A baker's son, who dreams of becoming a riding master at Vienna's Spanish Court Riding School, is admitted as an apprentice and achieves his desire under the tutelage of both two-legged and four-legged masters.
ISBN 0-689-71824-1 (pbk.)
1. Lipizzaner horse—Juvenile fiction. 2. Spanische Reitschule (Vienna, Austria)—Juvenile fiction.
[1. Horsemanship—Fiction. 2. Lipizzaner horse—Fiction. 3. Spanish Riding School (Vienna, Austria)—Fiction.
4. Horses—Fiction.] I. Dennis, Wesley, ill. II. Title.
PZ10.3.H43Wh  1994
[Fic]—dc20   93-34065

# 1. THE MORNING PARADE

THE clock on the steeple of St. Michael's church showed two minutes before seven. Hans, driving his father's bakery cart, clucked to Rosy to hurry. In two minutes they must be at the Hofburg. Rosy broke into a shambling trot, clattering over the cobbles at her best pace. And just as the church bells were chiming the hour of seven the policeman on the Josefsplatz threw wide his arms in a commanding "Halt!"

From both directions all cars screeched to a stop. Hans pulled up smartly. His body alerted, and a smile of eagerness spread across his face. His luck and timing had been perfect this morning. He and Rosy were not only first in line, but they were nearest the curb, too. The very best spot to see.

It was the Lipizzaners Hans was watching for, the famous white stallions of Vienna. Every morning they were led out from their stables on one side of the Hofburg, then through the archway to the great old Palace which housed the Spanish Court Riding School. Here they were carefully trained in the intricate and beautiful movements of classical ballet. And here each Sunday great crowds thronged the vast hall to see their unique performance.

Hans, the baker boy, had never been inside the Palace. He had no money for a ticket. But the horses fascinated him, and morning after morning he maneuvered for a glimpse of them in passing. From before daylight, while he splashed just enough water on his face to pass inspection by his mother, he

5

began scheming how to hurry her as she filled the big bakery trays with poppyseed bread and rye, long rolls and tiny *Kipferln*. On the rare occasions when she was ahead of schedule, he dawdled over his tasks of carrying empty flour bags and butter tubs to the attic storeroom. But when she was behind, he pitched in and helped feverishly, one eye on the clock. In his haste he sometimes dropped a kipferl, and once he clumsily let go a whole tray of hot bread. That day he ended up last in line, behind all the spitting, chuffing automobiles, and in the fog and fumes he couldn't see at all. But today, here he was in first place.

It was bitter cold this early February morning, but Hans was unaware of his cold fingers. The bright moment of his day had come. His eyes fixed on the great stable doors. They swung open. Even before he caught his first glimpse, his whole body vibrated to the kettledrum rhythm of hoofbeats on the cobblestones. First one vague shape emerged from the depth of the stables; then suddenly the semidarkness was slashed by a parade of white stallions, blanketed in red and gold.

"Notice me! Notice me!" Rosy neighed sharply. For a whisper of time the lead stallion glanced at the aged mare hooked to the bakery cart. Then he faced front, and in majestic dignity stepped across the street with long, supple strides. The other stallions never turned their heads.

Spellbound, Hans watched the rippling movement of the powerful hindquarters, the thrust of foreleg, the proud curve of the neck. A groom in dark uniform was leading each stallion, but he seemed part of the thick winter fog so that for Hans he did not exist at all. There were only the stallions, possessed of such power and nobility that Hans watched in a state of bliss as they crossed the street while all traffic stood still.

With their disappearance into the Palace, Rosy let out a whinny of yearning.

"Never mind, Rosy," Hans spoke to the old mare. "At least the biggest one noticed you."

The strident tooting of automobile horns set Hans in motion. He jiggled the reins and the old mare shook herself into action, ambling along at her own pace. She knew the next stop, and the next, and now that she had seen the white horses for this day there was no need to hurry.

Hans, born and reared in Vienna, accepted as his birthright the austere grandeur of the Imperial Palace; and he accepted the fame and beauty of the white stallions though he did not know the story of how they came to be in Vienna. When he first began watching them, he was satisfied with looking. It was an interesting event in his workaday world. He didn't mind being a delivery boy. In fact, some of the waitresses at the coffee houses were very nice and gave him treats of thick slices of sausage, which he much preferred to the baked goods his father made. And he even liked school, now that he was in the seventh year where history and science were full of daring and adventure. His world was small and ordered, and seemed likely to flow on quietly, like an arm of the Danube.

But lately as he jolted along, the old wagon creaking, Hans began to feel restless. He felt shut out when the great doors of the Palace closed on the mysteries of what went on within. Moved by an urge almost like Rosy's herd instinct, he felt he must join the white stallions.

"From the stable to the Riding School they go," he thought, "from one paradise to another. While Rosy and I just deliver today's bakery goods and pick up yesterday's trays, some washed clean, some spattered with whipped cream gone sour."

With his glimpse of the horses each morning, curiosity was building up in Hans. Now he watched the newspapers for accounts of the Sunday performances. Every picture of the Lipizzaners doing their ballet routines he clipped and saved. The names of the movements fascinated him. It was like another language. The *capriole*, the *courbette*, the *levade*, the *piaffe*. What did they mean? When was he going to find out what went on inside the great Riding Hall? How did the Riding Masters work the miracles he saw in the pictures? How did they make a great big powerful stallion stand up on his hind legs and hop along as if he weighed nothing at all? How did they get him to fly through the air like the winged Pegasus in his mythology book? How did they do it?

One night he cornered his father in the kitchen where he was braiding fat ropes of dough into bread. "Papa," Hans blurted, "could I go to the Riding School and learn to ride the white stallions?"

Before the man could straighten up and answer, Hans's mother handed him a shaker marked Poppyseeds. "Ach, Hans," she said, "never has there been a rider in our family. Or your papa's. The bakery business will be yours some day. Listen how nice it sounds: *Hans Haupt: Braided Bread a Specialty.* And when Rosy is gone," she added as if offering a premium, "you buy yourself a shiny new truck, yes?"

Hans seemed not to have heard. He watched the pastry brush in his

*Piaffe*

*Levade*

*Courbette*

father's hands as it slapped the melted butter up and down and across the fat cheeks of the braided loaves. Dutifully Hans shook the poppyseeds over them and watched them slither into place.

"Papa," he repeated, "could I?"

"Hans!" his mother scolded. "Not so thick! The seeds come high. The price is up."

Still there was no answer from the boy's father. Not until a dozen loaves were glazed and shoveled into the huge oven did he give his full attention to his son. Studying Hans's face, he wiped his floury arms and hands on his apron and settled himself into an old leather armchair in the living part of the kitchen. He nodded to his wife to leave the room. She picked up her bag of mending and obediently left. When the door had clicked shut,

Herr Haupt smiled at Hans in understanding and affection. "The truth is what you want, eh, Hans?"

"Please!"

"Well, then, you must remember who you are."

Hans shifted from one foot to the other; he hated long lectures.

"You come from a family of bakers, Hans. My *grosspapa,* my papa, your papa, and soon you. We are working stock. We do not venture behind the gates of palaces where great folks ride."

"But, Papa, maybe if I just looked inside to see how . . . "

"No one is ever satisfied with looking, Hans. It only builds the hunger. Like a starving man watching through coffeehouse windows, seeing people lift the forkful of strudel to their mouth."

He got up and roughed his hand through Hans's flaxen hair, as if now the query were answered and settled for all time. "Wash your mind of the white stallions, Hans. They are not for us; they belong to emperors and kings."

He chuckled softly to himself. "The life of a baker is not so bad. In a way he is an artist, too. Now, do your papa a favor and run to the tobacco shop and buy me a schilling's worth of my regular mixture."

On his way to the tobacconist, Hans joined a crowd of window-shoppers studying a lighted display of art collections. Among them were porcelain statues of the Lipizzans. They were so real-looking that just by squinching his eyes he could will them to life and make them jump clear across the window on their hind legs. In another window were red velvet saddlecloths bordered in gold, and saddles of leather so fine that Hans could almost feel their smoothness. Reluctantly he left the scene and bought the tobacco, his mind still busy with the horses.

Next morning at five minutes to seven he was slow-trotting Rosy past St. Michael's gate. If they let all traffic whiz by and if they hugged close to the curb, they could again be first in line.

## 2. ONLY A SCHILLING

HANS'S bedroom was on the second floor, above the kitchen. Depending on the hour, he could smell sugar browning, butter melting, almonds toasting, goulash simmering, coffee brewing. He was used to all these smells which told him the time of day. The room measured only eight feet by ten, but he liked it because it was all his. Once he had shared it with his sister. But since she had married a French baker and gone to Paris to live, he could sleep in her nice featherbed, and his old cot was stored among the flour sacks in the attic.

The walls of his room were painted a color that was neither yellow nor brown but a dull buff tone. "Just let me catch you pinning white horses on this nice clean wall and I'll . . . " His mother never quite said what the punishment would be, but the warning was enough. And so all that beautiful empty space went to waste. However, before she left, his sister, who was very pretty, had purchased an enormous mirror that covered almost half of one wall. Hans had poked fun of it at the time, but now it made a neat bulletin board. He had transformed it with pictures of the Lipizzaners. Some of the pictures were from newspapers, but these were not nearly so exciting as the colored ones from magazines. He had an arrangement with the news vendor near the Hofburg to sell him rain- or snow-damaged copies for a groschen apiece. Eagerly he brought them home and dried them on top of the oven. Once they were dry, he cut out each picture carefully, erased the

10

dirt, and with his mother's flatiron smoothed out the creases. Then he pasted the pictures up on his mirror. Now when he awoke each morning he was, for an instant, in the great Riding Hall—in a box seat, mind you—clapping in wild delight at horses leaping, horses rearing, horses dancing. And he saw the performance in all its glory. Then in the midst of his dream his mother's voice shrilled up the stairs. "Hans! Breakfast!"

But late in the day, back home after school, he had only to cross the threshhold to pick up the dream again.

Hans's schoolfellows regarded the collection with indifference, as something remote from their lives. They talked of soccer, and sailing on the old Danube, and bicycling to the Vienna forests, and hunting deer and hare in the mountains. Hans listened politely, then sooner or later he brought the talk around to the Lipizzaners. But unless at the same time he could offer warm pastries from the kitchen and hot chocolate with dollops of whipped cream, his friends found excuses to go home. Hans felt himself an outsider then. He could not join in their interests, nor they in his. No one but Rosy shared his enchantment with the white stallions.

As the brief morning meetings with the horses went on, Hans's curiosity mounted to the bursting point. Suddenly the not knowing what took place in the Riding Hall became intolerable. He committed himself to a bold purpose. He would no longer use the money he earned doing odd jobs at the coffeehouses to buy his own clothes. His mother was good at sewing. He would swallow his pride and wear his father's hand-me-downs. With the money saved he could afford a ticket to the Sunday ballet.

"Let him do it, Papa!" his mother urged one evening as she sat weaving a patch onto the seat of his school trousers. "Let him get this foolishness out of his head. Once seen, soonest forgotten, I say."

Hans warmed to her generosity. He leaned over and planted a kiss on the back of her neck so that she couldn't reach around and hug him. "Sure, Mama, that's all I want to do. I just want to see how they get those horses to leap and dance and do things that seem so unnatural. Maybe," he added, "I can even try out what I learn on Rosy."

His father looked troubled, but he did not object.

Next morning when Hans had finished his deliveries and was on his way home, the policeman on the Josefsplatz agreed to watch Rosy while Hans went into the visitors' entrance of the Palace to inquire the cost of tickets.

Facing the massive door, Hans paused, almost afraid to enter. A well-dressed man stepped in front of him and pushed it open. With a nod and a smile he waved the boy inside.

Hans stared at the businesslike look of the place. A wide aisle led directly to an enormous glass-enclosed office, and within it were a dozen or more girls busy at their typewriters.

Clutching his cap as if it might fly away, Hans approached the one open window. In awkward silence he stood waiting for someone to notice him. At last a girl with glinty red hair came over to the window.

"Yes?" She raised a question mark with her eyebrows.

In his best manner Hans had been rehearsing what to ask and how to ask it. Now he winced and dropped his cap, and in picking it up stepped on the bright shoeshine of the man behind him.

"Please excuse," he stammered.

The girl tried to conceal her amusement. "Come now, young boy. Did you want a ticket for some Sunday performance, perhaps?"

"Why, yes!" Hans said in astonishment. The girl had read his mind! "That is, no. Ach, I came to ask only how much is the cost."

"It all depends. The court loge, first row, would be twenty schilling. The first gallery lengthside is only five schilling."

"Five schilling!"

"But of course. Even so, we have no seats left for three months ahead."

Hans started to turn away when the girl spoke again.

"Why don't you just queue up, young man, and buy standing room in the second gallery? You can see as well from there; some think better. Then you just pay as you enter."

Hans took new courage. "How much is standing room?"

"Only a schilling. But you must come very early. Even at six-thirty in the morning the line begins."

The boy thought this over, a fresh new hope rising in him. One schilling he could save! He heard the man behind him cough politely and felt the nudge of an overcoat. Hans turned and smiled up at him. Then he ran down the corridor and out into the sunshine. He thanked his friend the policeman, climbed up onto his seat in the bakery wagon, and clucked to Rosy. Traffic shot past them as she clip-clopped along on the way home. Hans let the reins fall loose; he was figuring how long it would take before he could do as the girl said. "Just queue up and buy room in the gallery." In three weeks he could do it! Why had he not thought of it sooner?

## 3. FIRST IN LINE

THEY were happy weeks. It was early March and the city was stirring from its winter sleep like a bear that has hibernated too long. On week nights people were flocking to the Opera House, celebrating the birth month of Johann Strauss, the waltz king. On Sunday mornings they stormed the Spanish Riding School; in the afternoons they visited the parks and palaces.

Hans caught the heightened spirit of spring and took a streetcar one Sunday to see the Schönbrunn Palace of the Habsburgs, because he was studying about them in school. Unlike the tourists, he never set foot in the palace itself, but spent all of his time in the carriage house. The place was enormous! It held a hundred vehicles! Gingerly he fingered the coronation carriage of Napoleon, the carrousel of Empress Maria Theresa. There were all manner of carriages—golden chaises, chariots with tongues and spidery wheels of gold, and wagonets with neat folding steps, and barouches and phaetons, and splendid funeral cars in rich crimson and deepest black. And there was one stout excursion coach for mountain travel with even a toilet seat in it.

As he left the carriage house, Hans parted with five of his precious groschen to buy a set of colored postcards. They would be nice to illustrate the theme he was writing on the Habsburgs.

After his visit to Schönbrunn, Rosy's old cart seemed shabbier than

13

ever. But nothing could dim Hans's spirits. Spring and the incoming tourists meant more orders for buns and rolls, and more after-school jobs in the coffeehouses. The proprietors liked to have Hans around. "Nothing is too much for that boy," they bragged to their customers, "nor too little."

It was true. He heaved casks of pickles and apples to his shoulder and moved them from basement to kitchen. He sorted the hundreds of doilies that were used under every glass of water, under each and every plate. With a quick hand he layered the spotlessly clean ones to be used again, and tossed the others into a hamper.

His major task, however, was as busboy, a work he once loathed. Carrying mountains of dirty dishes had always seemed the worst kind of drudgery. But now, with a big tray held high, he felt like Atlas holding up the world. He exulted in his strength. He could feel his arm and chest muscles bulging and even his leg muscles hardening as he balanced himself in and out among the tables.

His schoolwork, too, showed a new zest. Each night after supper he hurried to the library to do his studying. It was easier to concentrate there. In his bedroom if his eye wandered, he was lost among the Lipizzaners on his mirror. But in the library his mind stayed put. Besides, there was Fräulein Morgen, the librarian, who often stopped by his table. "How are you getting along?" she whispered, so as not to disturb the other patrons. Often this came at the very moment he was butting his head against a seemingly insoluble question. It was a relief to pour out his problem to her. Like some genie she suddenly disappeared and as suddenly reappeared with an armful of books, each marked with a sliver of pink paper. Just by reading those pages he found the thing that puzzled him coming clear.

Some nights the books she brought were so exciting that he read on and on beyond the marked pages and Fräulein Morgen had to tap him on the shoulder. "Eight o'clock, Hans. Time to close the library." And so his schoolwork improved even as his pockets filled with groschen.

Already Hans had put a red circle around March 30th as his goal. By then he would have money enough to walk right up to the visitors' door and buy his ticket. His father had agreed to act as delivery boy on that Sunday morning.

"Creaky as my old bones are, I'll climb on the wagon and deliver for you," he said. "You have earned your treat."

14

On the last Saturday in March Hans had to buy new shoes. His old ones were beyond repair. But even so, he still had one beautiful schilling left!

And so at dawn the next morning he loaded the cart and hitched up Rosy. The day had arrived! He climbed up next to his father, watched the gnarled hands lift the lines and slap them against Rosy's rump. With a lurch the old mare took off, as if eager to have the business over with and to get back home.

The morning was dark and bitter. Pinpoints of snow rode slantwise on the wind. Herr Haupt pulled on his finger mittens. "Put yours on, too, son," he said to Hans.

The boy obeyed, even though his hands were still warm from the trays of hot bread.

Rosy's iron shoes rang noisily on the cobbled streets. No one was up and about, except a street cleaner, and a pair of lively dachshunds running

away with a fat man whose muffler snarled out behind him like the tail of a kite.

Hans laughed.

"Papa," he said, "today you won't see the white stallions crossing the Josefsplatz."

"So?"

"This morning even I won't see them cross."

"How's that?"

Hans laughed again for sheer joy. "Because they don't go out early on Sunday. That's why! They perform at ten and I'll be inside seeing them!" And he clapped his hands until Rosy caught his joy and broke into a trot.

As they pulled up in front of the Palace, Herr Haupt held on to

Hans's sleeve. "Look and listen for both of us, son," he said with a trace of wistfulness.

"I will, Papa. And I thank you with all my heart for doing my delivery work today."

Hans jumped out and faced the visitors' entrance. It looked big and remote, like a stage setting before the play begins. Not a soul was there. Not a soul in sight. He was first in line! Already he was savoring the prospect of seeing the stallions in action. He wondered what Rosy's friend, the biggest one, did.

The March wind sharpened with the morning, and the snow worsened as Hans stood there alone in the cold. Now he blew on his fingers through the mittens. When he stopped blowing, his breath made a hoar frost on the black wool and his fingers were colder than before.

To pass the time he did a kind of dance on the two stone steps that led to the entrance. And he ate the crescent-shaped rolls in his pocket.

At last the bells of St. Michael's chimed the hour of seven. Almost at once people began queuing up in little bunches as if the striking of the bells had hurried them. They came in two's and three's, and by whole families.

Only Hans seemed to be alone. He wished now he had saved enough money to bring his father too, but it had never occurred to him. He thought of his father as living behind his newspaper in a veil of tobacco smoke. He thought that his pipe and his bakery were all his father lived for.

The minutes wore on. The line stretched out until it was many meters long. But Hans knew there was no danger of his being turned away. He was *first*!

A group of teen-age boys on vacation from their school in Switzerland broke into a rollicking song. Everyone applauded them, to keep warm as well as to encourage an encore. The boys tried yodeling next, and Hans yodeled with them. Never in his life had he felt happier. All these people had come to see the only true horse ballet in the world. And he, Hans Haupt, was one of them!

Someone called out the hour. It was time for the doors to open. There was a quick silence of expectation. Then suddenly the morning air was torn apart with the sound of his own name screamed out.

"Hans! Hans!" It was his mother breaking through the line, sobbing hysterically. "Hans! Hans! Rosy is home, bleeding. And no cart at all. Go find Papa!"

16

## 4. WITHOUT THE DREAM

HANS was running now. He looked up at the cross on the little church of St. Michael's. He tried to pray, but he didn't know how to begin. He'd never needed help this desperately. He thought of his childhood prayer, but it didn't fit at all. He said it anyway as he ran:

"Now I lay me down to sleep,
Please, dear God, your child do keep;
Your love be with me through the night,
And wake me with the morning light."

He felt better then, and doubling his fists he ran with renewed energy. He knew the route. Down the Josefsplatz, past the library, past the Opera House, to the Sacher Hotel first. "My papa . . . has he been here?" he asked at the service entrance.

A man washing down the steps nodded. "Sure. Long time ago. What's the matter, Hans? Go on in. Cook will give you hot cocoa."

But Hans was whirling about, muffler and coattails flying. Out of the courtyard gate, out again onto the Sunday street. He ran fast, and faster, dodging the churchgoers, almost falling over the wilderness of silver-knobbed canes and umbrellas. An Italian chestnut vendor tried to stop him, to grab hold of his muffler. "They're hot. They're delicious," he sang out. "Only ten groschen a bag."

17

Hans broke loose, ran on. He flew past the windows of wax dummies, past the gallery of pictures. At crossings he dodged bicycles and motorcycles. He turned into the driveway of the Imperial Hotel and bumped into the head waiter, who was arriving at the same time.

"Boy!" the man snorted angrily. "Are you out of your mind?" He brushed his topcoat as if nearness to the panting, disheveled boy had ruined it.

Hans let out his breath in a gasp of pain. "It's my father, sir. I've got to find him."

A kitchen window opened and a waitress threw out a handful of crumbs for the birds. "Good morning, Hans. Come and help me fold napkins."

"My father," he called, "has he been . . ."

The girl's head was gone an instant, then popped out again. "Ja! Already your trays are half empty."

Eyes blinded by tears, Hans plunged on, flying along the Parkring from one coffeehouse to another. Always the answer was the same. "Sure, Hans. He's been and gone."

Almost down to the Danube canal, at the last coffeehouse on his route, Hans stopped and stared. Lying on a curb was a jumble of sticks and wheels. He would never have recognized it except for the blue letters of the word *Kipferln*. It was all that was left of the bakery cart.

A gang of boys were poking in among the ruins, looking for anything still fit to eat. Hans charged into them.

"Go 'way!" one yelled. "We were here first. You don't belong in our neighborhood."

"Just tell me what happened," Hans begged. "And where's the driver?"

The boys seemed not to hear.

"Didn't you see it?" he asked in desperation.

Now the boys felt important. They all spoke at once.

"Sure we did. What a crash!"

"Ja. A brand-new Mercedes hit the cart broadside."

"And the old man flew out like a bird and landed in that bush. See? It's all broken."

Hans knew his father was old, but he winced at the word. "But where is he?"

"An ambulance took him off."

One boy burst out in laughter. "What was really funny was that nag."

Now the others were convulsed. "No one could catch her," they guffawed. "She lit out like she'd been shot from a gun."

Hans turned for home. His lungs still ached. He couldn't run any more. He had to walk slowly, and with each step the burden of his responsibility weighed more heavily. In all Vienna, which hospital might it be? There was no way to know. All he could do was go home and try to calm his mother, and Rosy, too. Then to wait.

By the time he reached his own lane and stood in front of the narrow wedged-in house with the stucco falling off, he felt himself an old man, older than his father. He pushed open the door.

A policeman was already in the kitchen, explaining politely to his mother: "Dear Frau, no need for weeping. It's only one leg broken, and some bruises. Your husband can come home, maybe next week. Meanwhile," and he smiled at Hans, "you have a stout and dependable son here. Every morning at seven I set my watch by him. He goes to work the same time the Lipizzaners do."

The man in the Mercedes replaced the smashed cart with a shiny new one. But neither time nor money completely restored the father's shattered leg. His limping step dragged on the floor and up the stairs, a constant reminder of the accident.

19

Yet family life went on almost as before. Herr Haupt could knead and bake regardless, and Hans went on delivering in the early morning and studying by night in the library. It was a bittersweet pleasure to look at the Lipizzaners on his mirror or parading from stable to Riding Hall, for there was no one now who could drive Rosy on a Sunday morning, and what went on in the Riding Hall would have to remain a mystery.

One night when Hans came home from the library, his father was alone in the kitchen. He had turned off the electric light and was sitting in front of the window in a pool of moonlight, his leg propped on a stool.

"Hans," he said when the boy had hung up his jacket, "you and me—we must talk things out. There is something you should know. Come, sit down."

Hans felt a clutch of uneasiness. His father was a quiet man; he didn't believe in a lot of talk. This must be important.

"That accident," the father began, then faltered. He struck a match and lighted his pipe, taking longer over the job than usual. "That accident," he began again between puffs, "was my fault."

"Then why did the man in the Mercedes pay for Rosy's cart? And your hospital bills too?"

"He was rich, and he was kind."

"But how did it happen, Papa?"

The father leaned forward and spoke in whispered confidence. "Coming out of that driveway I . . . I dizzied."

"You what?"

"I dizzied. And next thing I hear a siren screeching, and I'm in the car making the siren noise. And it's an ambulance."

"Oh, Papa! I should have been driving."

"No, son, sometime it had to happen." He had more to say.

Hans waited.

"We are not rich, but we make ends meet, don't we, son?"

"Sure we do, Papa."

"Now look at it another way, son, and we *are* rich. We have great reserves—of will and strength."

The boy sat up straighter.

"So you try to cheer your mother. And no matter what happens to me, Hans, you keep on dreaming of the Lipizzaners. Without the dream you begin to die a little. And you are too young to die, yes?"

20

# 5. A MOMENTOUS CABLE

EXCEPT for a few scars that were responding to goose grease, Rosy was none the worse for the accident. She still whinkered to the white stallions each morning, and each morning there was the biggest one who glanced her way. But he and the others were totally unmindful of their effect on her and on the boy staring from the driver's seat.

At school the new term had begun, and homework doubled. At the coffeehouses the tables were busier than ever, now that the Lenten season was over. Hans worked from sunup to dark. There was no possibility of time off on Sundays. They seemed busier, if anything, than the other days. People seemed to eat more and oftener on the day of rest. So Hans could not queue up again at the Palace entrance.

The only really happy time came after supper when, with pencil and notebook in pocket, he ran to the library. He suddenly felt unbound and free. Free of the waitresses coaxing him to help with their work. Free of his mother's lecturing him to wear his rubbers, to wash his hands, to clean his fingernails, to do this, to do that.

Even at sight of the great National Library his spirits soared. High above the building, on an overhanging shelf of stone, the great god Apollo drove his four-in-hand across the face of the sky. The horses were bigger than life!

And once inside the library, Hans felt lifted into another realm. The ceilings were high-vaulted and frescoed in gold, with paintings of battles and crusades and angels and horses. And there were beautiful white marble statues in niches and on pedestals. The smell, too, was nice. Never any worrisome odors of butter burning, or almonds. Instead, the pleasant mustiness of old books. Best of all, in the library he had no sense of working when others were playing. All about him people were studying, too. All kinds of people. University students, looking like owls behind their dark-rimmed glasses. Rabbis scruffing their black beards as they read. Serene-faced nuns, their white hands turning the pages. It was like being part of something big and important. Maybe like playing in an orchestra.

One night when he had finished his homework earlier than usual, he began drawing from memory the statue of Apollo driving his fiery team across the heavens. At closing time he shyly presented his picture to Fräulein Morgen.

She held it in absolute silence. Hans's face reddened. Was it so poor she could think of nothing to say? Crooking her forefinger, she motioned him to follow her into an inner office. There she carefully tacked up his picture on a bulletin board which carried no other pictures, only a few typed notices.

"I like it!" she said, standing back to admire. "You have not traced it from a book. You do horses very well," she added. "Do you know, Hans, the reason for this particular piece of sculpture on the coping of the library?"

Hans shook his head.

"Well, a long time ago the ground floor of the library housed the horses of the Spanish Court Riding School."

"It did?" Hans asked in surprise. "No wonder I like it here!"

Fräulein went on explaining. "Later, Charles VI ordered a new wing built and an arcade to join it to the old stables. Today," she smiled, "two centuries later, traffic roars through this same arcade."

"I know!" Hans exclaimed with feeling. "I drive through it every morning just so I can watch the white stallions go by."

Fräulein nodded. "Often I have seen you when I come to work early. Once I even spoke to you, but you were so intent on the horses you couldn't see or hear anything else."

In sudden inspiration she began searching for something in her desk. Her fingers riffled along until they picked out a cablegram.

"My cousin from the United States was arriving in Vienna this week," she explained with a smile. "But today I had this cable from him from Washington. You see, he is a member of the President's staff and . . . Well, here, I'll read it to you." She unfolded it carefully and read: " 'Necessary to accompany President on inspection trip of new dams. Regret postpone holiday in Vienna.' "

"That is too bad," Hans said politely, wondering what this important stranger's change in plans had to do with him.

Fräulein was picking up a white envelope from her desk. "So now, Hans, if you can get away on Sunday, you may have the ticket he had ordered to the Ballet of the Lipizzaners. I myself have twice seen it."

All the blood left Hans's face. He felt sick, soul and bone. To have heaven offered and have to refuse it!

Fräulein waited, puzzled.

"I cannot get away," Hans said when he could speak. "My father cannot deliver for me. People eat on Sundays too," he added bitterly.

"Of course they do. But, Hans, do your deliveries take more than three hours?"

"No, Fräulein, but I have no time to wait in line."

"But you won't have to wait in line!" Fräulein Morgen stood up, and her laughter was gay as wind chimes. "Here, Hans, is a *reserved* seat! My cousin was given the best seat—in the very front row of the Imperial Box. You have only to be at the visitors' entrance by ten twenty-five." She got up and placed the envelope in the boy's hands.

Hans couldn't utter a word. He was afraid he might cry.

# 6. FROM THE IMPERIAL BOX

WHEN Hans told his mother and father of his good fortune, they exchanged looks of amazement.

"Think of it!" Mamma said. "A seat in the Imperial Box. Our boy!"

"Hmmm," Herr Haupt mused. "That man from America—he must be somebody important to get a ticket in the court loge."

"Oh, he is, Papa! He's right up next to the President."

When Sunday came, Hans finished his deliveries in double-quick time. Then he gave Rosy a once-over-lightly and an extra measure of oats. "Today I shall see your friend," he spoke into the whiskery ear.

He hurried into the house and found his parents in a happy mood— Papa yodeling as he had not done in years, and Mamma humming as she heated pails of water and polished his boots. "It's almost like a wedding!" she said. In honor of the occasion she opened a fresh bar of 4711 soap. "I've been saving this to bathe my grandson." She sighed. "But Jacques is already a big boy, and so far away in Paris; who knows when?"

Hans was bewildered by this change of feeling. Two months ago his mother was scolding, "Hans! The Palace is no place for baker boys!" Today she was urging him: "Scrub your ears. Brush your hair. Clean your finger-nails. Use the 4711 for the body, but pummy stone on your hands."

He was glad to escape to the bathroom and let the billowing steam envelop him. He tested the water with his big toe. It was just right and he

24

slithered into its warmth. It felt good. In spite of the whole hour he had left, he scrubbed in breathless haste. He must not be late.

By nine-thirty, his face shining and beet red, he shot down the stairs fully dressed and ready for inspection. His mother looked him over as if he and not the Lipizzaners would be on parade.

"You'll do," she said, bursting with pride. "You could rub shoulders with an archduke or even an emperor . . . and you smell better. Isn't it so, Papa?"

Sitting in his old leather chair, Herr Haupt nodded contentedly. Hans noticed with a start that his father's face seemed to have taken on the same creased leathery look. But the eyes under the wiry brows were smiling in triumph as he opened his hand and held out a two-schilling piece in silver.

Hans turned the coin over, studying it, not knowing how to say thank you. Then he shouted: "Papa! It has the picture of Prince Eugene on it! His statue stands by the Hofburg, and he's riding a Lipizzaner."

"I know. That is why I saved it for you."

"But, Papa, I don't really need it. Fräulein gave me my ticket."

"I know that, too, but a man of twelve should have a little money in his pocket. In case he wanted to buy a program. And maybe," he added wistfully, "maybe the truth is I just wanted something to give, so that something from me is there with you."

He stood up now and put both hands on the boy's shoulders, holding them tight. Gray eyes looked into gray eyes for a long moment. Then, "Hans," he said, "all Viennese are proud of the Lipizzaners. Even I who have never seen them. It is something wonderful we inherit from the past. But for most of us it is a thing to admire from afar. Like stars. Or the moon when it is new."

He let his hands drop from the boy's shoulders and he regarded him almost as a doctor examining a patient. "Son," he said slowly, thoughtfully, "I don't want this morning's experience to be so beautiful it will break your heart. It may be only once in a lifetime for you."

Hans thought of these words as he left for the Imperial Palace. He was touched by his father's concern. But as he walked along the Josefsplatz, excitement took over and the warning dissipated like mist when a fresh wind blows. He threaded his way in and out among the Sunday strollers, his mind on tiptoe. As he approached the Palace, he saw people coming toward him, away from the entrance. He overheard one remark, "And after waiting in line two hours, there's no room!"

Silently he thanked the man in Washington for the reserved seat, and walked right up to the visitors' door, his ticket held out. With fast-beating heart, he followed after an usher, climbed the stone steps, and took his seat in the front row of the empty loge overlooking the great Riding Hall.

He felt all at once on the brink of something deep and wonderful. He was here, actually here, about to see the mystery!

His eyes swept the quiet vastness. Below him and above, and all around, was beauty such as he had never imagined. The beauty crashed in on him—the whiteness of it—walls white as fresh snow, and stately white pillars marching around the balcony holding the gallery on their gold-encrusted shoulders.

The hall was enormous. It could hold a million horses, he thought. Yet somehow it was delicate, with crystal chandeliers hanging from the ceiling like fairyland. Stabbing through all this whiteness the morning sun worked magic on the chandeliers, shattering their crystal prisms into bits and pieces of color—blue and yellow and red. Hans marveled as his eyes tried to see it all. He wondered if even heaven could be so beautiful.

He looked below at the neatly raked earth on the floor. Was it pulverized clay like Rosy's stall? Sawdust? Sand? Or a mix of all three? It would be nice for horses' feet. And if a rider fell . . . he wondered, did they ever?

Now his eye studied the two posts in the very middle of the arena. What were they for? They were crowned with two Austrian flags, red-white-and-red. He noticed that they were fastened securely at the bottom. He knew this was good because when the horses came thundering in, the breeze they made would not ripple the flags and cause the horses to shy.

After a while Hans was conscious of sounds around him . . . people puffing up the steps, polite coughing and conversation, spectacle cases clicking open and shut, people sitting down beside him, behind him. Until now he had been too busy to look at his program. He took a quick glance at it. The performance might begin any moment, and he must know what to look for.

The first event was listed simply, "Young Stallions." Hans saw that the horses' names were printed in big bold letters, as if they were first in importance. And they each had two names. The riders' names, however, were printed in much lighter type, and their last names only. Hans chuckled. The horses were important here. So far everything was better than he had dreamed.

26

Before he could read on, a hush fell. Suddenly the music of violins and flutes, trumpets and cymbals rose and swelled until the hall was full of sound. Slowly the great double doors at the opposite end swung open. Eight snow-white stallions, their gold trappings gleaming, entered in single file. In majestic dignity they moved forward, between the flags, the whole length of the hall, toward the Imperial Box, toward *him!*

They were lining up now, eight abreast, right below him. Hans looked down and recognized each one—the Roman-nosed, the dish-faced, the ram-nosed. And the tallest one, Rosy's friend. His mane and tail were the color of old ivory, which made his coat seem whitest of all.

As for the riders, Hans was scarcely aware they existed, until the moment when in great solemnity they lifted their two-cornered hats and held them at arm's length in a courtly salute. Impulsively Hans stood up and returned the salute.

From then on the pageantry flowed before him like a dream. To the strains of lilting music the stallions waltzed. They marched. They did the cross-over. They stepped diagonally forward. They two-tracked. They pirouetted in platoons of four, in three's, in two's—as rhythmically as if they had been born to dance. Six events merged, one into the other, like sequences in a dream. Then the music stopped.

A silence of expectation hung over the hall. The moment had come for the "Airs Above the Ground." This was the mystery Hans had come to see! Eagerly he opened his program. There would be four stallions, he noticed, but there was no way to tell which horse did which aerial movement.

He leaned over the red velvet railing. Every nerve tense, he saw the doors open. He marveled at how quietly and calmly the stallions entered to the merry music of a Strauss waltz. Then as the tempo quickened, their walk and trot showed fire and animation. Suddenly the movements were happening in quick succession. One stallion leaped into the air, kicking out both fore and aft until it seemed he might split apart. Another took his position between the two pillars, and without any bodily motion, he trotted in place, lifting his knees to incredible heights. The third one who, to Hans's amazement, was chocolate brown, froze into a statue, balancing on his hindlegs. For long seconds he held this pose while the applause exploded.

Now the tall, ivory-maned stallion took center stage. Rosy's friend was the star! Crouching on his hindquarters, he reared up, and with a mighty leap he jumped into the air, and forward on his hind feet. The audience gasped as he propelled himself upward and forward again, his forefeet never touching earth. How could the hind legs support all that weight? Would they break? No, the stallion was doing it again!

All this while the audience watched in utter stillness. The only sounds were the faraway notes of flutes and the heavy breathing of the horse. Every sense alert, Hans was trying to see *how it was done*. How was the horse prompted? What were the magic signals? He could detect nothing. Without any stirrups at all, the rider was sitting ramrod-straight. He was like a chameleon; he hardly showed. Everything was for the glory and beauty of the horse.

As the stallion sank back to earth, the audience in both galleries rose as a mountain out of the sea, and the applause erupted in a thunder. Hans alone was unable to move. He was frozen in wonder.

He had seen it. It was real. But it was still a mystery.

28

# 7. VISITORS FROM STYRIA

HELD in the spell of the morning, Hans lagged home. He was not the same boy who had left the house a few hours ago. He had glimpsed another universe, and things could never be the same again. Questions were spinning around in his head. If only someone could give him the answers!

With his hand on the latch to the kitchen, he hesitated. He heard strange voices within. He started to turn away, but his mother had seen his shadow through the starched white curtain, and opened the door wide.

"Hans!" she cried. "See who is here—all the way from Styria. You remember Tante Lina and Onkel Otto?"

Hans remembered only vaguely. When he was a little boy he had visited them on their farmland bordering the Alps. Most of what he remembered was a plump Haflinger mare that let him trot and gallop her bareback. He nodded to his aunt and uncle, who were sitting in the company places at the table, and gave them a faraway smile. He didn't trust his voice, not yet.

"Well, Hans," his father prompted, "shake hands and give a greeting."

"Good-day," Hans said in a breathy voice he hardly knew as his own. Then to be polite he added, "How is your Haflinger?"

Onkel Otto laughed, deep and hearty.

"Ach, Hans," Tante Lina chided, "do you think nothing but horses?"

"Leave him alone," the uncle said. "He is dreaming." He turned his big jutty nose toward the stove, and with nostrils quivering like a bird dog, he sniffed the paprika goulash stewing in its own juice.

The table was set for Sunday dinner and everyone sat waiting for Hans to join them, waiting too for a full account of what he had seen.

"First, hang up your good jacket," his mother said to Hans.

Hans was glad of an excuse to go upstairs. He took as long as possible. When he came back down, clouds of steam were rising from the table, and every plate was mounded with goulash and dumplings.

"Well, boy?" Onkel Otto asked. "Can you tell us now?"

Everything that Hans wanted to say seemed locked deep inside him. Helplessly he looked at his father and stammered, "Oh, Papa, it was a sight!"

Tante Lina was pinning her napkin in place. "I've seen pictures of the Palace Hall," she prompted. "The chandeliers, Hans, I understand they have twenty thousand crystal drops. Do you think that could be true? And whoever cleans them?"

"I—I don't know."

"Were they lighted on a bright day like this?" she persisted.

"I don't know."

"Was there music?" the mother asked.

"Oh, yes, Mamma."

"Was it a big orchestra?"

"I—I don't know. I think it was hidden."

"Come now," Onkel Otto said, knifing a drop of gravy from his vest, "what in heaven's name *did* you see?"

Now Hans found his voice. "I saw the horses! But I did not see how it was done."

"How what was done?" the two men asked in unison.

"Papa! Onkel Otto! How do the riders make the stallions prance in one spot? How do they make them fly without wings? How do they make them jump on their hind legs?" There was no stopping him now. "The horses even walk different—on springs! And why is it called the *Spanish Riding School*? And why . . . "

"One question," the father said, "I can answer."

Hans put down his fork. "Yes?"

"The name is Spanish because the horses are Spanish," the father replied. "That much I know. The first ones came from Spain."

"Do they still come from there?"

Onkel Otto took a gulp of coffee and set his cup down with satisfaction. "I can answer that, Hans. The Lipizzaners now come from the Piber Stud Farm up in the mountains, right near us."

Hans bolted his mouthful of meat. "Then why," he asked, "are they called Lipizzaners?"

There was an embarrassed silence. Finally Onkel Otto dismissed the question with a wave of his fork. "One thing more I know," he said, taking a second helping of goulash. "The Riding School, Hans, was built for royalty, for the nobility who have the time to ride and study and learn. Not," he added with a wagging finger, "for the likes of bakery boys."

Hans's happiness was undimmed. He finished his dinner without knowing what it was he ate.

That night he lay wide-eyed in the darkness; he had so much to think about. Without knowing it, his uncle had struck a note of hope. If the Spanish Court Riding School was built for people who had time to study and learn, he would find the time, and Fräulein Morgen at the library would help him. Suddenly she loomed bright as a Christmas-tree angel. Tomorrow night he would begin!

# 8. CHEERS FOR XENOPHON

THE evenings now were not long enough. Hans and Fräulein Morgen entered into a plan of action. He would study his lessons the first hour. Then she would find a book on the Lipizzaners for him to read until closing time. Because she had given him the ticket to the ballet, she felt somehow responsible for his burning interest and was determined that a boy who hungered for knowledge should be given all he could digest.

"Hans," she said, bending over him so that he caught the faint fragrance of 4711 soap, "first make out a list of your questions."

"For my schoolwork? Or," his tone became eager, "for the Riding School? I already have made that out."

The patrons around the table looked up, some scowling, some smiling indulgently.

"Lower your voice," Fräulein whispered. "For your schoolwork first, of course."

Hans sighed. Why did what a person *want* to do always have to give way to what he *ought* to do? Fretting over the delay, he opened his notebook and showed her his school assignment. It read: "Our project this week is Ancient Greece. Select one of the following persons and write an essay on his contribution to modern civilization: Aristotle, the scientist; Homer, the poet; Hippocrates, the father of medicine; Phidias, the sculptor; Socrates, the teacher; Xenophon, the historian and general."

Unhesitatingly Hans pointed to the last name.

"Why him?" Fräulein whispered. "Why not Phidias?" She herself sculptured for a hobby. "We have some splendid material on his works."

Hans shook his head. "If Xenophon was a general, I figure he fought on horseback."

Fräulein nodded and disappeared.

Hans squirmed. Valuable time was being lost. He went over to the big dictionary. If he was going to spend a whole week on Xenophon and maybe have to read his essay out loud to the class, he should at least know how to pronounce the man's name. He lifted hunks of pages until he came to X. There were several long columns of frightening words—Xanthippe, xanthochroid, xenomorphic—until he came finally to Xenophon. "Zĕhn-oh-fun" it was pronounced. And before Hans could read the few lines about him, his eye pounced on a picture of the general on a black horse, standing on the shore of the Black Sea. Arms outstretched, he was giving thanks to the gods after a 1500-mile march with 10,000 soldiers.

Fräulein Morgen touched him on the shoulder. "Xenophon wrote many things," she said with a sparkle of discovery, "but this volume must have been written expressly for Hans Haupt! It is the earliest known work on the horse and his care."

It was a thin, morocco-bound book, with a gold medallion of a lion hunt on the cover. Hans hurried back to his table, and his pool of green light. He ran his fingers over the title embossed in gold: *The Art of Horsemanship.* Quickly he opened to the Introduction, and with the first sentence he clapped his hand over his mouth to keep from laughing aloud for joy. He read it a second time:

> *Seeing you are forced to meddle with horses,*
> *don't you think common sense requires you to see*
> *that you are not ignorant of the business?*

For the next hour Hans was swept back more than two thousand years in time and wisdom. To his amazement, he learned that Xenophon's cavalry rode without stirrups; yet they could command a horse to dance and balance on his hind legs exactly as in the horse ballet. What was more, Xenophon explained how it was done! Hans read the ancient words in a fever of discovery.

"When a horse bends his hind legs on the hocks and raises the forepart

33

of his body so that anyone facing him can see the belly, then you must give him the bit so that he may appear to be doing willingly the finest pose a horse can strike."

Now Hans was beginning to get answers! He started to take notes, then put his pencil behind his ear. Here was something he could remember without notes. He read on in breathless haste.

"Some, however, teach these maneuvers by hitting a horse under the hocks, others by telling a man alongside to strike him with a stick under the gaskins. We, however, consider that what a horse does under constraint he does with no more grace than a dancer would show if he were whipped and goaded. No! A horse must make the most graceful and brilliant appearance *of his own will,* with the help of gentle aids."

Hans wanted to stand up and cheer for Xenophon. His hands were sweating with excitement. He wiped them on his trousers before turning the next page.

"Whenever a horse chooses to show off before other horses," he read on, "he stretches his neck highest and flexes his head most. Looking fierce, he lifts his forelegs freely off the ground and carries his tail up. Therefore, whenever you induce him to carry himself as he does when he is anxious to display his beauty, you make him look as though he took pleasure in being ridden, and you give him a noble, fierce, and imposing appearance.

"We cannot too often repeat that after the horse prances in fine style, you must dismount quickly and unbridle him. Then he will come willingly to the prance the next time."

Leaping out on the next page, in almost startling reality, was a picture of Xenophon on a cavalry charger. The stallion—neck arched, eyes fiery —was balancing on his haunches, forelegs ready to flail the enemy. In a wide border around the picture were war horses in wildest action—flying downhill, uphill, leaping over walls, swimming streams, attacking in full combat. Hans eyed the page wistfully. He longed to cut it out and put it up on his mirror. Instead, he took his pencil from behind his ear, tore a sheet from his tablet, and painstakingly copied it all. He would make up his essay into a kind of book, and he would use this for the cover.

Lost in his drawing, Hans was unaware when people around him began gathering up their papers, and leaving. He did not even hear the guard call out the closing hour. Fräulein had to shake him back to reality.

Reproduced from *Histoire Pittoresque de l'Equitation*, by Charles Aubry.

"Hans!" she laughed. "I see you prefer your schoolwork tonight. Where are all those questions about the Spanish Riding School?"

Hans could only laugh, too. Sheepishly he handed her the crumpled list and watched over her shoulder as she read.

"How did the Riding School begin?

"Why are the horses called Lipizzaners?

"Where are the colts born?

"Why is one horse chocolate brown when all the others are white?

"How can the riders sit so straight?

"How do they make horses do such unnatural tricks?"

"Fräulein!" Hans exclaimed suddenly. "I want to cross out the last question. You see," he said, feeling important with his new knowledge, "the Lipizzaners are not performing tricks, they are doing natural movements—with the rider's help."

As he stepped out of the library that night Hans breathed deep of the cool night air. It was funny the way his world had suddenly grown big. Being sure of his goal made all the difference, he figured. The moon shed a gentle light on the Hofburg, making it look warm and mellow. He crossed over and walked around the Palace. Opposite the main entrance he stopped in front of the Prince Eugene monument. The horse bore a strong resemblance to Xenophon's charger, rearing on its haunches in the same pose.

All at once Hans was driven by a mad desire to sit a powerful creature like that. He looked to right and left. The street was quite deserted. In the darkness no one would see him. Quickly, before he could change his mind, he dropped his tablet in the grass. The pedestal of the statue had fluted columns and many ledges, some deep, some narrow, all seemingly made for climbing. Glancing about once more to make certain no one was approaching, Hans mounted, step on step, using the palm of his hand as a lever until with a bound he leaped up on the top of a column, onto an overhang of marble. To catch his breath he perched there a moment, holding onto an ornamental medallion. Just as he was reaching for the next level he heard footsteps—measured, slow. He froze against the marble and waited. It was a policeman, walking his beat. The man moved on without looking up. Now Hans took one final bound to the topmost ledge, grabbed the horse's bushy bronze tail, and pulled himself up and up until at last he sat on the wide cold rump. He inched closer to Prince Eugene, reached around him and took the reins in his own hands.

Erect as a rider in the Spanish Riding School he sat there, stone still. He looked down at the city and up at the moon, imagining he was in the arena, and the moon was a chandelier. And there in that moment all his yearnings crystallized. He made a choice for his whole life. He, Hans Haupt, would become a Riding Master in the Spanish Court Riding School. There would be no turning back now.

# 9. SO MUCH TO LEARN

WHEN he arrived home, there was no need to explain his tardiness. The kitchen was empty. He started for the stairs when he noticed his old cot from the attic standing against the wall. And piled on top of it, as if they didn't amount to very much, were all of the pictures from his mirror.

He took the stairs two at a time and tore into his bedroom. It wasn't his any more. Kneeling beside his bed was a curly-haired boy, saying Hans's childhood prayer with a French accent:

> "Now I lay me down to sleep,
> Please, dear God, your child do keep . . ."

The boy stopped in the middle, looking up in curiosity. Hovering over and around him were Hans's sister Anna and his parents.

Anna turned quickly toward Hans, and suddenly with tears and laughter she was almost suffocating him in a big hug, and explaining at the same time how sorry she was to put him out of his room. "It will be only for two years," she comforted, "until Henri gets out of the army."

"Two years!" Hans echoed, without saying it aloud.

Anna went back to the kneeling child, listening as the prayers went on and on with all the "God blesses" at the end: "Maman and père and grand-père and grandmère and Oncle Hans, and . . ."

Hans tiptoed downstairs and out to the little stable that was part of the house. It was bad enough to have to give up his room, but to a foreign

38

boy made it seem worse. A sob broke in his throat as Rosy, with a whinny of gladness, heaved herself up to greet him. To keep from thinking, he mucked out her stall fiercely and he gave her an extra measure of grain. Then hunching down, his back against the wall, his legs stretched out in the soft litter, he fell asleep to the rhythm of her chewing.

Anna found him there and shook him awake. "It won't be forevermore, Hans. Meanwhile, you and Jacques can be like brothers. He can help do some of your chores. And I will drive Rosy whenever you want a holiday."

Being an uncle at twelve to a shoulder-high boy made Hans feel suddenly old and trapped. Jacques clung to him as if he were his father, asking him to play catch, to help him with his schoolwork. Hans liked the boy, but he needed more time to think of his own future. Now the only bright spot in his life was in the evening, at the library. But it was three days before the household settled down and he could return there.

Fräulein greeted him as if he had been gone for weeks. Triumphantly she pointed to two big handsome books she had been saving. Hans noted happily that they were as full of markers as a porcupine is full of quills.

"Finish your essay first. Then," Fräulein smiled, "come for your dessert."

Hans was boiling with pent-up energy. He sharpened his pencil to a stiletto point. Then writing as fast as it would go, he told the story of Xenophon's exacting horse-care on the long ride from the inland of Asia Minor to the shores of the Black Sea. By the time he had finished he felt as if he were one of the ten thousand soldiers on that grueling march.

With the essay completed and fastened together with his drawing as a cover, Hans hurried to get the promised books. Fräulein handed them over as if she envied Hans. "You can see they are very, very old," she said, wiping the yellow-brown dust from her fingers. "The leather is crumbling and the bindings are loose, but these authors were the founders of the training methods used today. One book is in French and here's a dictionary to help."

Carefully Hans made a tray of his arms and carried the books back to his table. They were so big he had to stand up to read and turn the pages. The man sitting next to him obligingly moved over one seat to make room. All at once Hans felt like a digger of history. It was as if he had awakened these men from their slumbers to get up and teach *him!* He was fascinated by de Pluvinel, Horse Master to King Louis XIII. The great teacher seemed to be saying, "Hans! Listen and take courage! At seventeen I was already

Levade

Piaffe

Capriole

Courbette

a rider in 'above the ground' maneuvers. At twenty I was appointed Horse Master to the boy-king of France."

De Pluvinel proved as exciting as Xenophon. There were wondrous pictures in the book—one of de Pluvinel showing the king how a horse could be trained in aerial movements by working between two pillars. The pillars were exactly like the ones at the Riding School. Hans ran to show Fräulein.

"Look!" he exclaimed. "This man invented the pillars! Do you remember them in the Riding Hall?"

Fräulein nodded. "How could I forget, with the Austrian flag fastened to each one, and a living white statue between?"

It was a half hour before closing time, but Hans had to dip into the second big book. It was in the original French by Guérinière, written in 1733 "with the approbation and privilege of the king." Here at last Hans learned the names of the aerial movements and what they meant. No wonder they were French words! With Fräulein Morgen to help him translate, he discovered that Rosy's horse had done the *courbette,* which Guérinière described as a "leap in quick cadence on the haunches."

Hans thought back to the Sunday performance. The first aerial movement he had seen must have been the *capriole*. With painstaking slowness he translated, "In the capriole when the horse is in the air, he kicks out with as much force as if he wants to separate himself from himself."

The second horse, he now knew, had done the *piaffe*. The caption under the picture explained, "When a horse trots on the spot between the pillars and when he folds his arms high and gracefully, this is called the piaffe." Hans chortled at thinking of forelegs as arms.

The third horse must have done the *levade,* Hans figured, for certainly he had crouched on his haunches and reared up to a 45 degree angle.

He traced all four of the pictures to get them exactly right, and he labeled them according to Guérinière.

Night after night Hans read everything Fräulein could find about the Lipizzaners. His answers came thicker, faster. He learned that the Lipizzaners took their name from the little town of Lipizza near the Adriatic Sea, where originally they were foaled; that the name persisted, even though their foaling-place now was at Piber in the province of Styria. He learned that it was a good omen when a brown Lipizzaner was foaled. In years when there were none, disasters fell—war, fires, pestilence.

He learned all manner of unrelated but exciting things: that Lipizzaners grow up much more slowly than other horses, and live longer; that there were six founding sires of all present-day Lipizzaners; that the riders in the Sunday ballet doff their hats to the picture of Archduke Charles VI, who founded the school. Blushing, Hans remembered leaping to his feet to return the salute, as if it had been meant for him.

Only one thing he found hard to believe—that Lipizzan colts are born dark, some coal-black; and that gradually they lighten in color until they become the snow-white stallions he had seen at the Riding School. This he must see for himself. He still had the two-schilling piece his father had given him. It would help him to go to Piber. But how could he get away?

One day when the chestnut trees were bursting with buds and the grass was turning a soft green, Hans began to think how nice it would be at Piber. Already some of the colts would be born, and in his mind's eye he saw them skittering out of the barns, all knobby-kneed and wobbly. But were they really dark as night? And were they all dark, or did some have white blazes on their foreheads and maybe white socks or stockings? And in their play did the colts really dance and leap and take on the very poses of the horse ballet? Or was it a half-way thing, like parakeets who are supposed to talk but only their owners can understand them? If Anna meant what she had said about driving Rosy for him, then some Sunday he would go. If he was going "to meddle with horses," he could not be ignorant of their colthood. But he must go now, before the foals grew up.

When he told Anna his plans, she fell in at once with the idea. Life for her had been dull — washing clothes, helping with the baking, working on needlepoint bags to earn money. Driving Rosy would be fun. She would see the great city again, and mingle with people, and hear laughter.

Frau Haupt clamped her lips at the idea. "How will it look," she asked, "a pretty young lady, a mother, driving a bakery cart?"

Herr Haupt had quite a different concern. "Ach, Hans," he said, "why must you know so much? Why walk into a wall of heartbreak?"

But in the end it was Mamma who sensed Hans's need. "The boy looks pale. He should have a change," she said. "It will do him good, Papa. Let him go; even a cat can look at a queen."

And so it was arranged. Hans would take the train to the city of Graz. There he would stay overnight with Tante Lina and Onkel Otto, and the next morning he could go on foot to Piber.

41

# 10. TO PIBER!

SITTING bolt upright on the hard wooden bench, third class, Hans thought with a shiver, "This is me, *going to Piber!* I am me!" Excitement rose in him, so close to bursting he was afraid to talk to the other passengers for fear it might show in his eyes, or even in the burning color of his ears. He raised his hands and felt of them; they were fever hot. He remembered how his father used to call him Rabbit Ears whenever they went pink with excitement.

He was glad he had the seat next to the window and he gazed through his own reflection at the world rushing by. He wished the train would roll faster—get quickly to Wiener Neustadt, to Bruck, to Graz. Then he'd be there, almost. Again he felt like a digger of history, an archaeologist uncovering the ancient past. The mares he would see carried the blood of the Moor horses that had once raced across Africa, conquering tribe after tribe.

Eyes staring wide, he watched the suburbs of Vienna give way to woodland and plowland. He was overwhelmed by the bigness of the world. To pass the time he recounted the six Lipizzan dynasties, like an actor rehearsing his part. Pluto, Conversano, Maestoso, Siglavy . . . the names thrilled him. In time he would recognize one stallion from the other, saying, "This fellow is a Siglavy; note his dish-face. That one with the Roman nose is pure Maestoso." He grinned to himself, tickled at the idea of knowing so much.

"We're coming to a tunnel," the man beside him said. "It's like a children's toy tunnel. It doesn't go through a mountain or even a hill."

"Then why is it here?" Hans asked.

"Because Emperor Franz Josef liked tunnels, and so we have sixteen between here and Graz."

After that bit of information the stranger fell silent until, with a pleasant "Auf Wiedersehen," he got off at Wiener Neustadt.

The train began rolling upgrade now, winding among hills with vines staked out in neat rows, and now and again an ancient castle showing gray and craggy above pines and fir.

The rest of the trip was a succession of tunnels and bridges and hamlets, and winding valleys of purest green, and little streams rushing to join big rivers. At Bruck two rivers flowed together to form the wide, clean Mur. For a whole hour the train meandered along the river's course as though it might get lost if it struck out on its own.

It was twilight before the countryside gave way to the red rooftops of Graz. The city straddled the Mur like some giant. Hans recognized it at once by the enormous clock tower on the high hill. It dominated the city like an exclamation point. He remembered how on his last visit it bellowed the hours morning, noon, and night, and nearly frightened him to death when he was climbing its winding stairs just as the clock struck twelve.

Tante Lina and Onkel Otto were both at the station with a new pony cart and a new Haflinger, round and red-gold as a russet apple. Soon they were on their way toward the farm up in the hills, on the very road to Piber. Each mile brought Hans nearer his goal.

Sitting in the farmhouse kitchen, impatiently waiting for supper, he watched Onkel Otto draw a map on the back of an old calendar.

"It's a long walk to Piber," the uncle explained, sketching on his map a castle here and a church tower there. "If you will just wait until tomorrow noon, I will drive you there. I have business at the iron works nearby."

But Hans could not wait that long. He planned to start out at dawn. He bolted his supper of liver dumpling soup and apple strudel, and then began to yawn uncontrollably.

Tante Lina took him up to his room. Opening the wardrobe, she laid out a green jacket and a hat decorated with cock-of-the-wood feathers, shorts of deerskin, and long woolen hose.

"For me?" Hans asked in surprise.

Tante Lina nodded. "You may wear these tomorrow when you go walking to Piber; you'll look like a real Tyrolian," she said proudly. "I'll leave the hat on top of the wardrobe so the feathers won't get broken."

"And after tomorrow can I take them home with me?"

"Of course. They belonged to a neighbor boy, but he's outgrown them and I've mended and cleaned them so no one will ever know they've been worn." She rubbed her hands happily. "You like them?"

"Oh, yes. You don't know, Tante Lina, how nice it is to have a boy's suit to wear instead of . . . "

"I know. Instead of your papa's."

There was a smile between them.

Moonlight washed into the room. In the big featherbed, Hans waited for sleep that would not come. He shut his eyes and even then he saw the moonlight on the striped tail feathers of the woodcock. He heard the door to the other bedroom close. Suddenly he burst out of bed. He could not wait until morning. He dressed in his new clothes and, holding a hobnailed boot under either arm, he tiptoed downstairs under cover of Onkel Otto's snores. He tore off a corner of his map and left a note on the kitchen table:

*I've got to go tonight. Thank you for everything*
*Hans*

The moon splatter-painted the hills and valleys. Hans had gone only a few steps when he felt something whir across his face and settle on his shoulder. He stifled a scream, then very gingerly turned his head and looked eye-to-eye at an owl. The owl had no intention of leaving his warm perch, and Hans felt less alone as he settled down for the long walk. There were stretches of field on either side of the road and the stacks of last year's hay looked like butter kegs with the churning stick poking up into the night.

Hans liked the night. Maybe he belonged to it, he thought, like foxes and owls and rabbits and nightingales. He liked the rustling of trees, and bells tinkling softly as the cows grazed in the white fields. And the deer would be awake, too. Only the brown wooden farmhouses were asleep under their thatched roofs.

After a while the owl winged noiselessly away. In a moment Hans heard the thin terrified squeak of a mouse. He tried to tell himself that the owl was helping the farmer save his grain, but all at once he hated the bird, and he brushed his shoulder where the creature had sat.

Dark shadow piled on darker shadow as a grove of trees blackened the road. Hans walked faster to get out into the moonlight again. The air chilled as he climbed higher. He hunched his shoulders into the warm jacket and climbed ahead with long strides, scanning the hills for his first landmark. He must have been walking for an hour, perhaps more, when suddenly and with startling clearness came the sound of hoofbeats and the creaking of wagon wheels. He flattened himself against a tree trunk as the hoofbeats came closer. Then around the bend, red-gold in the moonlight, a plump Haflinger was jogging toward him at a brisk trot. Hans raised his voice in joyous recognition. "Onkel Otto!"

Hans never remembered the rest of the trip. He slept in the straw in the back of the cart, under a heavy buggy robe that smelled old and good.

## 11. THE FOALING PLACE

AT THE foot of the hill to the Piber Stud Farm, Onkel Otto shook Hans awake. Half-dazed with sleep, he took the rucksack of lunch Tante Lina had sent along, mumbled his thanks, and said good-bye. For a long moment he stood uncertainly at the bottom of the path, looking up at the centuries-old castle and the red church tower with the dark pines standing like soldiers behind them.

In the misty light of morning the scene reminded him of the paperweight he had at home. When you shook it you made snow flurries, and through them you could see a tiny castle and tower. Suddenly he was sharp awake. He brushed the straw from his jacket, finger-combed his hair, and slung his rucksack over his shoulder. Then he climbed the path that made two gentle switchbacks, then rose steeply up a carriageway and out upon a courtyard. With scarcely a glance at the castle and church on his left, Hans headed straightway toward the stables.

A row of children, looking like a flock of birds on a telephone wire, were perched on the top rail of a paddock fence. They sat facing a long barn, waiting expectantly as if for a show to begin. The very air seemed charged with suspense. Hans did not have to wait at all. At that moment, right before his eyes, the red doors of the stable creaked open, and from the dimness within, out spilled a herd of mares and foals. With a catch of his

46

breath Hans leaned over the fence, gaping at what he saw.

It was true! The mares were dazzling white. And tagging at their heels, as orderly as shadows, were their foals, some inky black, some rusty black, but all of them dark against the startling white of their mothers.

"It's true!" Hans smothered a cry. It was as though he had seen the herd in a dream and now they were real after all!

The children jumped off the fence and ran flying down the lane toward home. For them the show was over. For Hans it had just begun. He made himself part of the closely packed bunch of mares and foals trotting out to meet the morning. They were barefoot, and their hoofs made only a small thunder on the road as they climbed uphill toward their grazing meadow. They paid him no attention. He might have been one of them, or he might not have existed at all.

Two grooms, who went along as shepherds, waved Hans a friendly welcome. Hans felt little shivers race up and down his spine; it was wonderful to be part of this crisp, golden morning. Running, taking big steps to keep up, Hans noticed that many of the foals had white stars on their foreheads, and blazes too. He sighed in happiness at his knowing all about them—how their coats would gradually gray, and in time their markings be lost in their white grown-upness. He spied one bright bay colt among the black, and in a flash he remembered what he had read at the library. He was glad there was a bay one. This year nothing dire would happen. There would be no war. No epidemic. Again the feeling came over him that he had dreamed all this, and now it was real.

When the cavalcade, snuffing and snorting, reached the grazing meadow the close formation fell apart in an explosion of joy. The foals ran squealing from their mothers only to rush back at them, bunting them in fierce play. Two chesty colts put on a private boxing match, standing on their hind legs, flailing the air with their forelegs, never landing a blow. Others pranced and leaped and kicked out like the stallions in the Sunday ballet. The bay staged a race all his own, while his mother ran after him, nudging him back into the fold. The mares too felt the bigness of their freedom. They cut undignified capers, rolling over and over, rubbing their backs and their cheeks against the cool grass.

Hans wanted to join in the sport, to do cartwheels, to spread-eagle into the lush greenness, to shout across the world, "It's all true! Every bit! The colts are doing courbettes and caprioles for fun!"

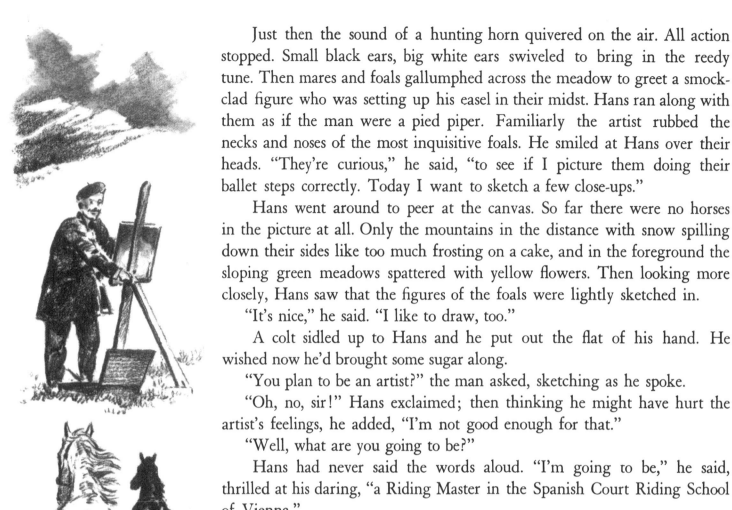

Just then the sound of a hunting horn quivered on the air. All action stopped. Small black ears, big white ears swiveled to bring in the reedy tune. Then mares and foals gallumphed across the meadow to greet a smock-clad figure who was setting up his easel in their midst. Hans ran along with them as if the man were a pied piper. Familiarly the artist rubbed the necks and noses of the most inquisitive foals. He smiled at Hans over their heads. "They're curious," he said, "to see if I picture them doing their ballet steps correctly. Today I want to sketch a few close-ups."

Hans went around to peer at the canvas. So far there were no horses in the picture at all. Only the mountains in the distance with snow spilling down their sides like too much frosting on a cake, and in the foreground the sloping green meadows spattered with yellow flowers. Then looking more closely, Hans saw that the figures of the foals were lightly sketched in.

"It's nice," he said. "I like to draw, too."

A colt sidled up to Hans and he put out the flat of his hand. He wished now he'd brought some sugar along.

"You plan to be an artist?" the man asked, sketching as he spoke.

"Oh, no, sir!" Hans exclaimed; then thinking he might have hurt the artist's feelings, he added, "I'm not good enough for that."

"Well, what are you going to be?"

Hans had never said the words aloud. "I'm going to be," he said, thrilled at his daring, "a Riding Master in the Spanish Court Riding School of Vienna."

There! He had said it! He had said it right out. He sighed, almost hysterical with relief. In his mind he saw the great Palace in Vienna and the eight snow-white stallions doing the quadrille, and he was one of the riders—not thinking of the audience at all, only wanting to be trusted and understood by the one creature he rode.

For a long time the artist did not speak. Why should he break the news to the boy? He wasn't the boy's father. Let him go on with his foolish dream. "What's your name?" he said at last.

"Hans. Hans Haupt."

"Where are you from?"

"Vienna. My father has a bakery, and I drive the delivery cart."

The man put down his brush. "There's a vast difference between a cart-horse and a Lipizzan."

"Oh, I know."

50

"It's a long apprenticeship; it would take years and years. By the way, how old are you?"

"Thirteen. And I graduate next year from school."

"Well, young fellow, when you're sixteen, you'll have forgotten all about this."

Hans shook his head. Never had he felt so sure of anything. A mare nudged him and he scruffed his fingers underneath her mane. "I've decided!" he announced. He didn't trust himself to say more.

At eleven o'clock, when the mares and foals went back into the barn for their noon siesta, Josef, the younger of the two caretakers, sidled up to Hans. "If you want," he said shyly, "I could spend my noontime with you. I could show you about."

"I'd like that!" Hans beamed.

Josef was a solemn, quiet lad who seemed to recognize in Hans a strong fellow feeling. He explained things timidly, in little half-sentences, as if he thought Hans already understood. Sometimes he only pointed. In the weaning barn he shrugged and smiled wistfully at the row of weanlings tied along one wall, getting used to eating wisps of hay, getting used to being away from their mothers. There was a pitiable cross-fire of nickerings, but both Hans and Josef knew that it was part of growing up, that the colts would soon be reconciled to the separation.

In the mare barn Josef pointed with pride to an enormous blackboard with the names of each broodmare and the date she had foaled or was yet to foal, and the sire's name too. And he showed Hans the loafing barns where the mares-in-waiting munched their hay together, drank out of the same trough, and dozed and daydreamed, waiting for their colts to be born. And he showed him the high-crested stallions in their stalls, not acting fierce at all. And he took him into the tack room with its rich soap-and-leather smell, and showed him old saddles and bridles and stirrups used by famous stallions.

"This one," he said, pointing out a scrolled saddle, "belonged to Franz Josef's favorite stallion, Florian. And this bridle was worn by Maestoso Borina when he lived here for a year to sire some colts. He is now the champion courbetteur of the world. He can jump ten times, successive."

"Ten times!"

"Ja. That is a lot, no?"

Hans mulled over the name. Maestoso Borina! Wasn't that one of the

51

names on the program he had at home? Could it have been Rosy's friend, who did the courbette? He must look when he got back.

At noon the two boys shared each other's lunch. Hans's rucksack held meat wrapped in a cabbage leaf and the apple strudel left from last night.

"I'm a cheese-eater," Josef said, offering his mother's homemade cheese and buckwheat bread.

They ate sitting in the garden of the churchyard, leaning up against the wall and looking out to the valley ringed around by the snow-piled Alps. Hans supposed it was a cemetery they sat in, but the markers were cemented into the wall. One showed a life-size knight in armor kneeling in prayer, his ringed hands in supplication, his sword sheathed at his side.

After lunch, Josef led Hans through a deep Red-Riding-Hood forest and out upon an upper range where graying three-year-old colts were trotting and galloping.

"They're getting strength in their bones and hoofs," Josef explained. "When the weather gets warmer, they won't even come in at night."

"But they're still so playful," Hans said.

"Ach, why not? They have the summer yet, all to themselves. Not until fall do they go to school in Vienna."

By the time Onkel Otto called for Hans in mid-afternoon, the two boys were fast friends.

As Hans climbed into the cart, Josef touched his sleeve. "Someday I will come to Vienna," he said with his shy smile, "and you can show me how you train in the Riding School."

Hans nodded. He did not doubt that the time would come.

Onkel Otto clucked to the mare, and she took off downhill as if she could hear the rustle of oats. Hans turned and looked backward, watching until Josef and the stables and the castle and finally the church tower were swallowed up and lost to distance.

When Piber was quite out of sight, Hans breathed a deep sigh of contentment. "Things are working out just fine, Onkel Otto."

They rode on in silence, each busy with his own thoughts.

## 12. THE IMPERIAL STABLES

ONE Sunday soon after his visit to Piber, Hans was sorting out the horse pictures that had been taken down from his mirror. He was in Rosy's stable, preparing to tack them up on the wall opposite the door. In the midst of his sorting he came across the program he had saved from the performance in the Riding School, and he sat down in the straw to enjoy it all over again. Suddenly his eye was drawn to the fine print at the bottom of the page which had somehow escaped him.

> After the production it is possible for visitors to inspect
> the stables opposite the Riding School until the hour of 13.

Why had he not seen this before? Oh, but he must hurry! It was already past twelve. He dumped the pictures into a box, put them on the high windowsill out of Rosy's reach, filched some of her sugar he kept hidden in her cart, and without bothering to change clothes he ran all the way to the Hofburg, winking at the Prince Eugene statue as he rushed past.

Within the cobbled courtyard he stopped a moment to catch his breath and to let departing visitors pass by. He was glad they were leaving. He didn't want to be part of a group of chattering children, and women talking baby-talk to majestic stallions that could do more dance routines than any of them. Then, still breathless, he entered the cool, softly lit stable.

Again he had that curious sense of having been here before. It wasn't just the familiar smells. It was a sense of belonging here, and to Time. For

centuries the stable must have looked exactly like this—the clean-swept brick corridors, the row upon row of shiny mahogany stalls, the halters hanging above each one, and within each stall a royal stallion, white as the snow on the mountains of Piber.

He looked down the aisle and mentally swept the few visitors aside. In their place he saw Charles VI walking grandly, gesturing with his jeweled hand, pointing out the talents of each stallion. Sweat broke out on Hans's forehead. He wanted to rush from stall to stall, lead this one out, lead that one out, put them through their paces right here in the corridor.

Someday *he* would be pouring oats into those white marble mangers. Someday *he* would be lifting down the gold-ornamented bridles, putting them on carefully, according to Xenophon's instructions. He missed nothing. The name plates fascinated him. They were big and important looking, framed in shining brass, and he noted that each bore a double name. Usually the top one ended in "o," so that must be the sire's name, he figured; and the bottom one in "a," so that must be the dam's.

When at last the aisle was cleared of people, Hans stepped forward. Now he could get acquainted with the horses. He felt in his pocket for the little sack of sugar and offered some to Pluto Ancona. The stallion momentarily turned around, eyed Hans impassively, then went back to his oats.

The stablemaster, a grizzled man with big, strong hands, saw the little incident. "Ja, ja," he laughed. "They are like people. Some are friendly, right away. And some take years. Seldom they make a strong attraction to a stranger. Herr Hofrat says there is a chemistry between people, and between horses and people."

"Who is Herr Hofrat?" Hans asked.

"Who is Herr Hofrat!" the man repeated in astonishment. "Why, that is our title of respect for Colonel Podhajsky."

"Oh, I know *him*."

"You do?" The stablemaster arched his eyebrows in surprise.

"I mean," Hans stammered, "I saw him in the big Sunday performance. The stallion he rode acted as if he were carrying"—Hans blushed—"as if he were carrying God."

"That was Neapolitano Santuzza, a great *caprioleur*. You're right, he does think that." The stablemaster looked at his watch. It was past the hour of thirteen, but he was in no hurry and he liked this eager boy. "Perhaps you wish to know about the names," he offered.

"Oh, yes!"

"We use a kind of shorthand," the man said, "to represent the six lines of stallions that go back to the founding sires. Every Lipizzaner here in the school descends from one or more of them." He took a scrap of paper from his pocket and made little symbols on it to explain the dynasties:

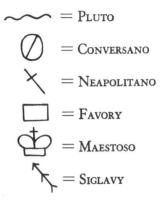

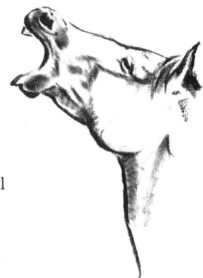

Hans asked for the piece of paper to keep. Then he went on from stall to stall, meeting the horses in turn.

"This one's got Arabian blood, hasn't it, sir?"

"How do you know?"

"Why, the dished profile, the small ears."

The stablemaster nodded, impressed with a thirteen-year-old who knew so much. He added what the boy did not know. "In the Sunday performance he does the levade. He holds his pose for fifteen seconds."

The stallion sniffed at Hans's offer of sugar and with a snort blew it away. Then he tossed his head high and curled his lips. It was almost a sneer.

"It's nothing personal, boy; they've had so much company today."

The next stall bore the name Maestoso Borina. Hans stopped in his tracks. This was a name he knew! The champion *courbetteur!* He must have seen him day after day, at the archway. He must have seen him from the Imperial Box. He had touched his bridle at Piber. Now he was about to meet him, face to face.

Hans wiped his hand and shook some fresh sugar into it. A champion like him, he thought, wouldn't want sugar that had been snuffled all over by somebody else. Before thrusting his hand between the bars he made a small chirruping sound. Maestoso Borina turned his head slowly to look at the boy.

55

Hans gasped in surprise. It was Rosy's friend! The same one!

With his deep, dark eyes the stallion was studying Hans. Then graceful as water swirling he came closer. Hans stood stock still, lost in the moment of looking, and being looked at. He pressed his upper arm tight against his body to hide the tremor of his hand. And he talked softly until Maestoso Borina pricked his ears. He inched closer. Now at last the feelers touching Hans's fingers, then the pink muzzle, then the sugar gone. Dark eyes still studied the boy as the munching went on, slowly, savoringly. For some time they smelled noses, breathing in each other's breath.

"I congratulate you," the stablemaster said soberly. "You have made friends with the champion courbetteur of the world. His record is ten springs into the air before he lands again on his forefeet."

Hans's eyes never left the stallion's.

"We do not call him Maestoso Borina," the stablemaster continued. "We call him by the one name, his mother's. *Borina* we say, the way you speak of Mozart or Strauss."

Hans nodded. "I don't mind his having a feminine name at all. He's so big and powerful, no one could mistake him. How old is he, sir?"

"He, my friend, has twenty-four years, but he is still a good springer, and the pride of the School. He is the last one of all these stallions to be born at the Royal Court Stud of Lipizza."

"*At Lipizza!*" Hans gasped. Why, this was like meeting up with history!

"Ja, at Lipizza. Come, I show you." The stablemaster unlatched the stall door and beckoned Hans inside. "Now you will see how his whole pedigree is branded on his body." Proudly he traced the L on Borina's cheek. "This of course shows he is a Lipizzaner. Now look closely at his barrel."

Hans's heart was hammering in his chest. He knew he was going to ask to touch the brands.

"Here under the saddle," the stablemaster went on, "is the M to show that he is by a Maestoso sire, and directly below is the symbol which tells that his dam was sired by a Conversano stallion.

"And now, boy, come look at his hip. Trace for yourself the royal crown and the L for Lipizza, where he was born."

Hans winced as he fingered the crown, wondering if it had hurt Borina when the branding iron struck.

The stablemaster laughed, divining his thought. "No, it happens so quick they don't feel it." He looked at his watch, gave Borina an affectionate pat on the rump. "I must lock up now," he said, as if he were sorry. "You come back another Sunday."

He accompanied Hans to the door and held out his hand in good-bye. Hans put his inside the rough, calloused palm. He felt the fingers close around his in a clasp so strong it made him blink. His heart warmed. He would like working for this man when the time came.

All the way home he whistled happily. He knew he was being silly, but he couldn't wait to tell Rosy that her friend was a champion, that he came from the original Court Stud at Lipizza!

# 13. SUDDEN CHANGES AT HOME

HIS hand on the kitchen door, Hans was thinking, "Now in the mornings when the stallions are led across the street, I'll always recognize him. Maestoso Borina! What a nice special name."

His thoughts cut off sharply. On the other side of the door a man's voice was saying: "No more stairs. Better he sleeps on the cot right here in the kitchen. And no more coffee, and no tobacco."

Abruptly Hans came back to reality. He heard a satchel click shut, and knew without looking that the satchel and the voice belonged to old Doctor Obermeyer, and he knew he was speaking of Papa. The boy stood stricken. The last sentence was like a death sentence. Papa without his coffee and pipe would not be Papa at all.

Turning away, not wanting to be seen, Hans fled to Rosy's stable. There in the steaming warmth he hid his face in her neck and poured out his grief in uncontrollable sobs. How could he have been so happy when, at the very moment he was meeting Borina, Papa had been so sick?

Later, it was only Papa who could comfort him. "Hans," he said, "I'm going to be just fine down here in the kitchen. Why, I can boss Mamma and Anna without doing any of the work myself. And we'll borrow another cot, and if I have a spell of dizziness you'll be right here to give me my medicine." He smiled. "Hans," he said, "I love you, and you are all I have left of the future."

It worked out just as Papa said. Another cot was set up in the kitchen, head-to-head with Hans's, and often the man and the boy had whispered confidences in the dark before dropping off to sleep. Hans enjoyed this new companionship with his father. One night he said, "Papa, you'll never guess it, but I'm teaching Rosy to seek the bit and collect herself."

"Ach, Hans, don't talk a foreign language to your papa. It makes no sense. How can Rosy collect herself?"

"It's hard to explain, Papa. You got to get her hindquarters under her body, so she is collected and ready."

"Ready for what?"

"To walk or trot, or whatever you want her to do."

Herr Haupt shook his head. He was puzzled but proud. He was beginning to realize that Hans's understanding of horses was more than a boy's hobby. "Hans," he said, "I was wrong, what I said about baker boys. For you there is more to life than the bakery business. It is useful, but this other . . . maybe you should do it. Don't be afraid, Hans. You keep on believing."

As the days passed, Papa seemed to get better. And as he grew stronger, Hans went on with his planning. Almost every Sunday he visited the Imperial Stables, and after the visitors were gone, the stablemaster often allowed him to brush Borina's already immaculate coat.

On weekdays Hans worked with Rosy. He had found an old ramming rod from a muzzle-loading rifle, which he sewed down the back seam of his jacket. This made him sit very straight when he drove Rosy, and it made him think about improving her way of going. She was almost twenty now, and too old to try aerial maneuvers, but why couldn't she dance a bit? Perhaps learn how to trot on the spot, like the Lipizzaners?

He began working with her in the little stableyard behind the house. With Jacques and Papa watching, he tied Rosy between two wooden clothes posts. Then he pretended he was de Pluvinel, the great horsemaster of old, and that Jacques was the boy-king of France. By explaining what he was trying to do, it seemed clearer in his own mind.

"You see, your Majesty, Rosy must lift each foreleg high and hold it in the air a moment before setting it down again."

"Why must she?"

"Because, your Majesty, when you make your public appearances she will look as if she is treading on air, and you yourself will appear magnificent."

Jacques burst into laughter. "Rosy walk on air?"

Papa suppressed a grin.

"De Plume! Or whatever your name is," Jacques commanded with arms akimbo, "show us how!"

Hans was prepared. He had cut a birch switch one day when he was driving along the Danube Canal. Now he brandished it. Rosy was in no way disturbed, but Jacques screamed, "Don't hit her!"

"Tch, tch, your Majesty. The switch is only a prompter. See? I touch it behind this knee and it makes her lift her leg high. Now I do it to the other knee. See?"

"Why is she tied up, Hans?"

"I am not Hans, your Majesty."

"Well then, Mister Horse-Master, why *do* you?"

"Because the posts help train her. They keep her from trotting forward or backward, so the only direction she can go is up. Now do you see?"

"No, I don't see," Jacques said candidly.

But Herr Haupt nodded. He did.

In a matter of months shaggy old Rosy could do a fair imitation of the collected trot. It was a sight to behold. People stopped in amusement to watch the elderly mare, her knee action high and energetic, but hindquarters dragging. Hans asked her to do it often, hoping that sometime Herr Hofrat of the Riding School might spot them in the streets of Vienna and

say, "Who is that boy who can teach an ordinary carthorse the movements of dressage?"

And someone in the crowd would reply, "Why, sir, don't you know? He is Hans Haupt, a horseman of great promise."

And Herr Hofrat would reply, "Send the boy around to me. At once!"

But a whole year passed and no word came.

One early morning when Hans was ready to carry out the bakery trays, his father said, "I am tired. So tired." And he slipped off into death, like a fallen leaf drifting downstream.

Anna's husband, Henri, came home from the army on the day of the funeral, as though word had somehow reached him. His two years in the service were over.

The moment he dumped his bags on his father's cot, Hans disliked the man. He wore a clipped black mustache parted in the middle, and his hair was parted in the middle too and lay flat and shiny on his head, like patent leather. He had a way of smirking whenever Hans tried to speak seriously to him. "Little boy!" he'd say. And he had an irritating way of slapping his thigh, like an exclamation point to every remark.

Henri took charge of the bakery as if it had been pre-arranged. Even Mamma accepted him and fell in with his plans. She gave up her bedroom to Anna and Henri, and asked Hans to move back to his old room and share it with Jacques. She herself would be satisfied with the cot in the kitchen.

Hans rebelled at everything. It seemed like a sacrilege to sell Henri's French bread and croissants along with Papa's *Semmeln* and *Kipferln*. And whenever Hans entered the kitchen, he felt a pain and loneliness. Papa had been his friend, his confidant. Now Hans wanted only to escape.

"For a few weeks only I will stay," he told his mother. "Tomorrow, Mamma, I will begin teaching Jacques and Anna to take over my route."

"But what will you do?"

"I am fourteen now. Soon I will graduate from school."

"But where will you live?"

"I will go to the Spanish Riding School. And live there."

His mother nodded in resignation. She had known all the time, and Papa had known too, that Hans was not going to be a baker. Then as an afterthought she asked, "But, Hans! What if they don't take you?"

Hans had not heard.

## 14. THE WORLD IS A WHEEL

THE day after his talk with his mother, Hans presented himself at the office of the Spanish Court Riding School. His determination made him miraculously calm. The same red-haired girl who had once told him to queue up left her desk and came to the porthole.

"Yes?" she asked.

"My name is Hans Haupt. I wish, please, to see the Director of the School, Colonel Podhajsky."

"Have you an appointment?"

"No, miss."

"He is very busy. There are two men in his office now."

Hans's composure was suddenly gone, and with it his voice.

"Could I be of help?" the girl smiled.

"N-no. Y-y-yes. I don't know."

"Come, come," her tone was big-sisterly, "speak up."

"C-could I see him tomorrow afternoon?"

"No. Tomorrow he goes to Piber."

Hans was desperate now. "When *could* I see him?"

"I don't know. Perhaps if you told me your purpose?"

"I — I want to be a Riding Master," he said helplessly.

The girl hesitated. A strange resemblance between this boy and her own younger brother made her say, "Wait a moment." She clip-clopped on her high heels to her desk, studied an appointment book, and returned. "You come back a month from today," she said. "Here, put your address on this card, and if you do not hear from us, you be here at four o'clock on the tenth day of June."

For Hans the next month was one of minute preparation. He cleaned out his wardrobe, giving a bundle of clothes and a pair of shoes to Jacques. He gave him his precious collection of horse pictures. He taught Jacques the niceties of handling Rosy — how she didn't like being groomed under her belly, but liked a good rubbing wherever the harness leathers had touched her, how she submitted to the hoofpick if she were busy eating her grain. And he showed Jacques the technique of arriving at the Hofburg at the exact stroke of seven. One morning he pointed out Borina with great pride.

"Humpf!" sniffed Jacques. "He looks just like the others."

"Is that so? I suppose you think all children look alike, too."

"No, I don't. I know boys from girls."

At school each day and at the library each night Hans worked with single-minded purpose; he had to make sure he would graduate. He longed to tell Fräulein Morgen of his appointment with Colonel Podhajsky, but he decided against it. Better to surprise her.

Each evening when he reached home he was afraid to ask his mother if any word had come from the Riding School. So he never asked. But as the days melted one into another, Hans felt safer, surer.

June tenth came. A day of bright sunshine and a sky of deeper blue than Hans could believe. A good omen, he thought, as he arrived at the Hofburg. He was sure of it when he stood before the glass-enclosed office and the red-haired girl remembered him. "Come this way," she smiled.

Hans followed her down a long stone passageway that made a left turn and suddenly opened out into a room that looked like an art gallery. Hans stepped over the threshold in awe. The room was elegant with statuary, and with horse paintings illuminated by hidden lighting. It was so beautiful it seemed unreal. Only Colonel Podhajsky was real. He was walking around the center table as if he were striding out his thoughts. He seemed taller than Hans remembered. Tall and forbidding. In the midst of his pacing he swiveled on his heels to regard Hans.

The blood pounded in Hans's ears. It was so noisy he feared the Colonel might hear it.

Then the Colonel's face suddenly was friendly. "A boy who has waited

a month should have a hearing. Now then, Hans Haupt, state your business." He sat down at the table and waved Hans into the chair opposite.

The moment the Colonel spoke there was a strange thumping sound in the room. Hans glanced in the direction it came. And there stretched out on a golden sofa lay a dachshund, her tail wagging like a metronome.

Hans took courage. If a dog and horses liked a man, a boy had nothing to worry about. He stood up in respect. "Your Highness," he said, " I wish to be a Riding Master. I can start at once."

A twitching at the corner of the Colonel's lips was the only answer. After an eternity he asked, "And what experience have you had?"

"I drive a bakery wagon for my fa . . . " Hans winced. "That is, I did."

The Colonel's eyes sharpened. He had heard reports of the bakery horse and one day had watched Rosy with amusement. "Is it a blue wagon?" he asked.

"Yes, sir."

"And the mare quite aged?"

"Yes, sir. But she's lively as ever."

"How old are you?"

"Fourteen and a half."

With a kindly smile the Colonel stood up. He put a gentle hand on the boy's shoulder. "You come back in a year, eh?"

"But, sir!" Hans cried. "I'll do anything. I'll rake the sawdust in the Riding Hall. I'll sweep floors, polish brass. I'll muck out stalls. Oh, sir, it would be a privilege to clean Borina's stall."

"Why only Borina's?"

"Oh, I would do the others, too. Only Borina—already he likes me."

"Driving a cart horse, Hans, is quite different from working with Lipizzaners. I myself am still learning."

"Yes, sir. Even Rosy is still teaching me. But sir, I know a lot about Lipizzaners." The clear gray eyes challenged the stern brown ones. "Ask me, sir! Ask me anything!"

The Colonel mused. Yes, it would be a good way to end the interview. He fired his questions like beebee shot.

"Why are they called Lipizzaners?"

The reply was instantaneous. "Because they were bred at Lipizza."

"Who was first to teach the art of *haute école?*"

"Why, that was the Greek general, Xenophon."

"What does *Arbeit über der Erde* mean?

"Work above the ground, like flying and leaping."

"You understand it takes time to teach these unnatural tricks?"

Hans laughed weakly. He was sure of himself now. The Colonel was trying to trip him. "The little colts at Piber do these same movements naturally," he said.

The Colonel did not change expression. The rain of questions went on. "How early do you begin training a Lipizzaner?"

"At three and a half years."

"Why so late?"

"Because Lipizzaners grow up slower and live longer than other horses."

The bombardment was suddenly over. The silence in the room grew heavy. Hans cast about wildly for something to say. "They even teethe later!" he added in desperation.

The Colonel made a steeple of his fingers and studied them thoughtfully. At last he said, "I am impressed with your knowledge, Hans. You have knocked upon my Austrian heart. However, I cannot make an exception. Come back in a year, but even then I can make no promises."

"Herr Hofrat! Excuse me, please!" It was the secretary's voice. "The Herr Direktor from the Opera is here to see you. It is most urgent, he says."

Hans made his legs walk out of the room. He heard the Colonel's voice saying, "Make a note of the boy's name. Something about him . . ."

Hans did not stop to listen. He stumbled past a portly gentleman on his way in, past the girls in the office, and out into the cool afternoon shadows. He suddenly felt gutted and empty, like a building that had been bombed. The words would not leave his ears: "Come back in a year, but even then . . ." He was wrenched by his failure. There was nothing left in life. He could not bear to go home.

Slowly his feet took him to the library, but not to his usual place. He wanted to hide. No one would think to look for him in the magazine room. In deep misery he sat down among the old men dozing over their newspapers. He sat there for a long time. Just staring.

After a while, an old man nudged him with the pole on which his newspaper was clamped. "Want to read this one?"

Hans shook his head. He could not see for tears.

"Ja, ja, son. I too come here for comfort. 'The world is a wheel, and it will come round right.' You'll see."

# 15. SPECIAL ASSIGNMENT

WHILE Hans was in the depths of despair, sitting among the tired old men in the library, Colonel Podhajsky was having a jolly visit with the Direktor of Vienna's great Opera House. The two men were old friends. Each admired the other, and all Vienna admired them both.

After the handshaking and the first pleasantries were over the Direktor, a roly-poly man, lowered his weight carefully into one of the delicate baroque chairs. His steely eyes glinted and his tongue brushed his whiskers as if already he were tasting the success of his plan. "Alois," he began familiarly, "it is June! A time for love and laughter, a time when tragic opera should give way to gaiety and happy endings. And so," his shiny-pink face broke into a beatific smile, "we next play 'The Girl of the Golden West.'"

"I know," the Colonel nodded. "The American opera. We have tickets, my wife and I."

"Good, good! Now comes the reason I am here." The Direktor leaned forward until the fragile chair gave a squeak of protest. He went on, unmindful. "The beautiful Madame Jeritza will be the star." Here he kissed his fingertips and blew the kiss heavenward. "And in the last scene she must sing her final aria while sitting on a motionless white horse."

A smile played about the Colonel's lips. He began to suspect what his visitor had in mind.

"Could it be . . . " the Direktor pulled out a snowy white handkerchief

66

and blotted the beads of sweat on his forehead, " . . . that you would lend us your courbetteur, the one who can make so many jumps on his hind feet?"

The Colonel frowned ever so slightly. "Why Borina?"

"Because that fellow should be so tired by night he would stand still as a statue. You see, Alois, while Jeritza is an accomplished horsewoman, she forgets all else when she sings. It would be most embarrassing if, because of a nervous horse, she came a cropper before five galleries of her fans!"

The Colonel laughed heartily. Then his face grew serious. He walked thoughtfully over to the sofa and sat down next to his dachshund. His friend, the Herr Direktor, was asking a great deal. After all, Borina was a star in his own right. He was accustomed to order and routine. Besides, theaters were drafty places. Dangerous, too, with electric cords to stumble over, and people flying around waving scripts and moving scenery.

Herr Direktor wisely did not interrupt. Intently he watched the Colonel's face.

"On the other hand," the Colonel was thinking, "I never like to stand in the way of my children's success. Borina has great histrionic ability." Aloud he said, "Hmmmm. This could be a new star in his crown."

The Direktor smacked his lips in glee.

"But," the Colonel shook his head, "I have no extra hand to stay with him backstage, to watch over him like a mother, to keep him out of drafts . . . "

"Perhaps, Alois, all it needs is some trustworthy boy to lead him the short distance to the Opera House. As we are barely three hundred meters away, Borina would be in the streets for moments only. Another thing, Alois, offstage Madame Jeritza would devote herself wholly to him. She admires Lipizzaners so greatly."

"Hmmmm," the Colonel mused again, "I will have to consult with my stablemaster. He may know of someone." The Colonel stood up abruptly. "You will hear from me in the morning."

It was long past the evening meal when Hans finally went home from the library. His place was still set at the table and the lentil soup was being kept warm for him. Young Jacques greeted him excitedly, waving a square envelope which he had snatched from the table. "Look, Hans! Open it!"

Frau Haupt was excited too. "It came by special messenger!" She took the letter from Jacques and propped it against Hans's napkin ring.

67

Hans's eye caught his own name, and up in the corner the two words, *Spanische Reitschule*. His heart raced madly. Whatever the letter said, he wanted it all to himself. His mother read his mind. "Anna and Henri have gone to the Kino to see an American picture," she said. "And Jacques is going to help me hang fresh clean curtains in both bedrooms. Come, Jacques, we go upstairs."

"I don't want to! I don't want to!" The boy's voice mounted as he was pulled up the stairway, then faded as a door clicked shut.

Hans reached for the letter. He opened the envelope and took out a sheet of white paper. In the moment of delay before he unfolded it, he breathed a prayer. Then alone in the glare of the naked electric bulb, he read the few lines, read them over again. They were not like typewritten words at all; he could hear the Colonel's deep, vibrant voice saying them:

```
          Dear Hans Haupt,

     We have a temporary assignment which might
interest you. That is, if you feel fully capable of
walking Maestoso Borina to and from the Opera House
for the duration of the forthcoming production.

     The stallion is to be onstage a short time
only but will need constant watchfulness. Rehearsals
are to begin at once. Therefore, we must hear from
you at once.

     In view of the great responsibility which
would be entrusted to you, we will require a
letter of recommendation from a respected citizen
of Vienna.

     I remind you again that the assignment is
temporary and of a very exacting nature.
```

It was signed with the beautiful flowing signature: *Podhajsky*.

For one alarming second Hans's knees gave way. Then joy surged through him. He longed suddenly to share it. "Mamma! Jacques! Come!"

Jacques nearly fell down the stairs in his haste, and his grandmother was not far behind.

"Look!"

He held out the letter for them to read, to share in his glory.

Afterward he raced to the library. Who else but Fräulein Morgen should write the letter of recommendation?

# 16. BORINA'S CUE

WHEN Hans and Borina started out on their operatic career, it was as natural as two streams flowing together on their way to the sea. They formed an immediate partnership. Borina of course was senior partner, for he was much the older, but they both acted like a pair of boys off on a holiday. And indeed they were. Hans was graduated and out of school, and Borina was excused from morning sessions for the time being. So the world was all fresh and new for both of them.

Proudly that first morning Hans led his snow-white charge down the Josefsplatz, past the library, and to the Opera House. He felt they were in a world apart from ordinary citizens going about their ordinary duties. He wouldn't have been surprised in the least if someone saw a golden halo above them as they marched down the cobbled square and around to the stage entrance of the Opera House.

Herr Direktor greeted them enthusiastically. "Good morning! You are Hans Haupt?"

"Yes, sir."

"And your stallion — I forget how he is called. I think of him only as the great courbetteur."

Hans thrilled to the words *"your stallion."*

"His name is Borina, sir."

"On the program we will print his full name. You will carefully spell

it out for me." The Direktor produced a notebook from his pocket. He licked the point of his pencil, waiting.

"M-a-e-s-t-o-s-o  B-o-r-i-n-a."

In a flourishing hand the Direktor wrote down the name. "Now then, listen sharply. Borina plays in one scene only, but it is the grand climax of the whole opera."

Hans's eyes opened in astonishment. "The grand climax?"

The Herr Direktor nodded and resumed. "Riding Borina, Madame Jeritza enters the forest scene just in time to save Ramerrez from being strung up on a tree."

"Sir, who is Ramerrez?"

"He is chief of the outlaws and he is in love with Jeritza. As his dying request he pleads to the hangmen, 'Let my pure sweetheart never hear of my shameful death; let her believe I have fled to freedom.' "

"But does she save him, sir?"

"Of course. Thanks to Borina getting her there in the nick of time. Remember, Hans, when Ramerrez sings his last sustained note, that is Borina's cue. I must warn you," he added, with a waggle of his finger, "that the tenor, Ramerrez, is very temperamental. You must not cut off his song before he is through. Now we will rehearse." And he led the way to the great stage.

After only a few rehearsals Borina knew his cue as well as any two-legged actor. Herr Direktor reported the news to Colonel Podhajsky.

"Why wouldn't Borina perform well?" was the Colonel's retort. "He has a fine ear for music! Has he not been dancing to the waltzes of Johann Strauss, and the minuets of Mozart and Beethoven, for years?"

At each rehearsal the routine was the same. Well in advance of Borina's cue, Hans saddled him and gave Madame Jeritza a leg up. There she waited, refusing Hans's offer to hold onto the bridle. At the exact moment when Ramerrez concluded his plea, Borina bore her onstage. Watching from the wings, Hans was in a delirium of pride and joy.

Both he and Borina fell in love with the opera and with their new friends. Sopranos and bassos, violinists and horn blowers, electricians and stagehands chatted with them, and often brought treats to Borina. But always they consulted with Hans first.

"Hans, can Borina eat an apple from my lunch?"

"Hans, would licorice upset his stomach?"

70

"Would he eat a slice of torte, Hans?"

Even the Herr Direktor when he brought tiny peppermints from home would ask, "Has Borina had too many sweets today?" And only with permission would he offer the treat.

Hans was flattered to be looked upon as a veterinarian. He was responsible for Borina's health and safety, and everyone knew it.

Thus the first week of rehearsal went by in a routine of happiness. Hans walked his charge to and from the opera building each day, and he did a few stable duties at the Riding School. Often he found himself humming tunes from the opera as he worked. But he carefully avoided Borina's cue song, of course. He knew he had never been so happy before.

In the second week Hans felt a pinprick of uneasiness. He noticed that Borina waited for his cue in such eagerness that when he went on, his flanks were slick with sweat. It was almost as if he were afraid Ramerrez might be hanged before he could get there. The nearer it came to opening night, the more eager he became. Each time he made his entrance a fraction of a second earlier, so that Ramerrez had to cut off his final note while he still had plenty of breath left. This made the man furious. He swore loud oaths in Italian. He even stopped bringing nougats to Borina.

At the dress rehearsal things took a catastrophic turn. Borina charged onstage two full measures ahead of time!

Ramerrez grew livid. The whole cast froze. A deathly silence closed around them. It was as if lightning had struck and everyone waited breathless for the thunder. It came in a crash. Herr Direktor banged his fist on the piano and made a hideous jangle of sound.

Into the sudden quiet that followed came the hail of rage: "Hans Haupt! Come out here!"

Like one hypnotized, Hans moved ever so slowly until he stood downstage.

"Me?" the small voice asked.

Now the barrage let loose. "What kind of groom are you! You are a know-nothing!" The Direktor clenched his fist, then rubbed it where it had hit the piano. "Tonight we open. The house is sold out. *Do something!*"

"Y-y-yes, sir," a smaller voice said.

Hans quailed. A cold perspiration broke out all over his body. He was trying desperately to think, grabbing at straws of ideas. He whispered to Madame Jeritza, who was sitting rigid on Borina as if she were glued there, "Should I run back to the Riding School for a lunge-line so I can hold Borina from the wings?"

She shook her head vigorously. "The white strap would show."

Hans was growing frantic. His whole future hung in the balance. Never again would he be trusted.

Suddenly his eye fixed on a strip of green carpet in the wings. It was used to deaden the sound of Borina's hoofs backstage. Forgetting he was a stableboy, Hans yelled to a prop man who was perched on a ladder hanging leaves on the trees. "Can I have this piece of carpet?"

"Sure! I got more."

His heart pounding, Hans quickly rolled up the carpet. "This will stop Borina, sir," he explained. "I'll lay it in his path all rolled up like this. Then tonight I won't pull it aside until the very end of Ramerrez' song."

Herr Direktor spoke through tight lips. "See you don't!" His tone was icy cold. "Colonel Podhajsky will be here tonight, and if you ruin my opera, he will be sorry he ever laid eyes on you."

72

# 17 . SPECTACULAR ENTRANCE

IT WAS five minutes before curtain time. Hans tiptoed onto the opening set. Through the peephole, his eye swept over the theater . . . the main floor, the three rows of boxes, the five galleries. He was hunting for one person — Colonel Alois Podhajsky. Hans had to make certain he was there. After the performance, he told himself, the Colonel will come backstage and he could say, "Hans Haupt, you have handled your assignment extremely well. When the opera closes I want you to stay on at the Reitschule and become a Riding Master. In fact, you may begin at once."

Hans blinked. He was almost blinded by the dazzling lights and the glitter of gold, tier upon tier to the ceiling. Suddenly, as he looked, all heads began turning in one direction and white-gloved hands made a spatter of applause. The Colonel, handsome in black full dress and white tie, and his wife in furs and jewels were entering their box in the middle of the house. The Colonel bowed deeply, pleased and surprised at the ovation.

Just then the call boy shouted, "Curtain! Curtain!" In quick succession the house lights dimmed, the footlights came on. Hans flew into the wings, past the little groups of nervous actors, to Borina's stall. He found the great placid creature eating hay, completely undisturbed by all the chaos. He seemed to know it would be a long time before Act III. He stopped eating a moment to smell noses with Hans, then stood quite still while Hans

73

hand-rubbed his coat and combed the ivory mane and tail for the fifth time that day. Working eased Hans's nervousness, and Borina responded with little grunts of contentment.

As the first act gained momentum, Hans found himself stroking in time to the music and humming along with Madame Jeritza as her clear soprano voice came floating back to them. Borina nodded and dozed until Ramerrez sang his first love song, but even then he showed no signs of excitability. By the burst of applause that followed Act I, Hans could tell it was a success.

Act II, however, seemed never-ending. Horse and boy began pacing up and down and around the stall, passing each other at every lap. All the while Borina's ears were constantly at play, as if trying to pull out a melody meant for him alone.

It was a relief when stagehands began shifting scenery and Hans knew the second act was over. He brought out the Western saddle and the gem-studded bridle, and tonight he timed himself very carefully, allowing a full half hour before he saddled and bridled and led Borina into the wings. Maybe that had been the trouble before; they had always been too early and Borina had become over-eager with waiting.

The moment had come. It was time for Madame Jeritza to mount. Hans cupped his hands as a stepstool, and in one motion she swung gracefully into the saddle. She took the reins, settled herself securely, and nodded to Hans to place the rolled-up carpet in front of Borina. Then she leaned at the boy, giving him a dazzling, everything-will-be-all-right smile.

Hans returned the smile. He stepped aside, and with one eye on Borina he watched the action onstage. He saw the hangmen lower the noose, and he heard Ramerrez pour out his passionate plea, "Oh, let her believe I have fled to freedom." Confident that tonight Borina would give him full time, the tenor's voice rose and swelled in a tumult of emotion. He sang more eloquently than Hans had ever heard him.

Just as his final note faded, and just as Hans was about to pull the carpet away, Borina rose up on his hind legs and stood almost perpendicular. Instinctively Jeritza grabbed his mane as the stallion leaped over the carpet and landed onstage in a perfect courbette.

The audience gasped at the sheer beauty and audacity, then broke into a thunder of applause and bravos. It was the most spectacular entrance of Jeritza's career!

Without thinking, Hans bolted toward the stage to rescue her in case Borina should try another leap. But someone caught him by the seat of his pants and jerked him back into the wings.

In all the commotion, onstage and off, Borina was the only calm one. With great decorum he settled down on all four feet and stood motionless, waiting for his gentle rider to burst into song. With amazing self-possession, she did. Tremulously at first, then with growing ardor. She put into her aria such soul-stirring appeal that Hans closed his eyes, listening as if she were pleading his cause rather than the outlaw's. He leaned against the wall, his heart bursting in misery. Now all was lost. The Herr Direktor would be quick to tell Colonel Podhajsky whose idea it was to roll up the carpet. His career as a Riding Master would be over before it began.

He heard the curtain going up and down while Madame Jeritza took her bows. In his anguish he mistook the crescendo of applause as an expression of sympathy and understanding. He felt a dull pain in his chest. His spirits had hit bottom.

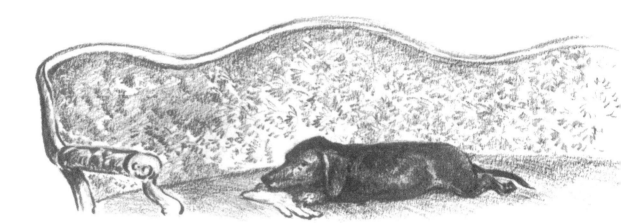

# 18. A NEW WORLD FOR HANS

IT CAME as no shock when the stablemaster next morning told Hans he was wanted at once by Herr Hofrat in his office. A strange girl ushered him wordlessly down the stone passageway and into the beautiful reception room. She left him alone, except for the dachshund, who looked up with half an eye, then went on snoring, her head resting on the Colonel's white gloves. Again she was a source of comfort. Hans longed to go over and touch her, but he restrained himself and sat down gingerly on one of the gilt chairs.

He thought of Rosy, and of his family, and he longed to crawl away and sneak home. He failed to hear footsteps on the carpeted floor until the Colonel was standing almost in front of him. Hans leaped to his feet, his face reddening. There was complete silence in the room.

Then Colonel Podhajsky suddenly laughed out loud. "Ja, ja, Hans," he said, his dark eyes twinkling, "I would not have missed last night's performance for all the coffee in Vienna."

"Sir?" Hans's mouth fell open. "S-sir?"

The Colonel looked at the boy's stricken face and realized what was troubling him. "Ach, Hans," he said quickly, "Borina's unexpected performance was a sensation. The papers are loud in praise of him. It was a great triumph for Madame Jeritza, too. The audience seemed to share it."

"But what about the Herr Direktor?" Hans stammered. "Is he not furious with me?"

The Colonel's laugh was deep and hearty. "Is ever a director displeased if an audience demands ten curtain calls?"

"Then I am not fired?"

"On the contrary! My message to you comes from both Madame Jeritza and the Herr Direktor. Now that she knows what to expect from Borina, you are to roll up the carpet each night."

"And after the opera closes?" Hans swallowed hard. "What then?"

It seemed that the Colonel had not heard. So dead a silence hung in the room that the ticking of a tiny gold clock sounded like hammer strokes. The Colonel turned to look at the hour, then without a word went over to the sofa, gently lifted the dachshund's head and retrieved his gloves.

Hans stood rigid, waiting.

"The Reitschule will be closed for the summer," the Colonel said at last. He pulled on his gloves, taking longer than necessary. After an eternity he added, "Yes, you may report for training in the fall. The first of September comes on a Monday. You be here the night before. Then we shall find out if Hans Haupt has the endurance and courage required."

Hans accepted the warm handclasp. Looking at the Colonel, seeing the future, he felt a frightening joy.

The summer dragged by in an agony of waiting. Hans had to work for Henri. He went back to the delivery cart while Jacques had a summer of play. Occasionally Hans caught a glimpse of the white stallions being exercised in the outdoor arena between the high walls of the Hofburg. But it was disappointing. There were no aerial maneuvers at all. A groom simply rode one horse and led another alongside, and they just walked and jog-trotted as if they were all on vacation.

The days fell away. July spun itself out. The first two weeks of August seemed without end. But of a sudden, as though someone had ripped the pages off the calendar, the summer was gone.

On the eve of September, with his few clothes neatly packed in his father's old brown satchel, Hans presented himself at the Reitschule.

Kurt Wagner, one of the apprentices, took him in tow. They had spoken to each other before, but now Hans felt himself scrutinized by a pair of sharp eyes that seemed to be measuring him for muscle and stamina.

"Come this way." Kurt turned on his heel and led Hans up dark stairs that circled steeply. Together they entered a long, sparsely furnished room.

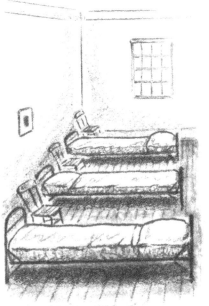

Three iron beds were lined up against one wall, with a plain wooden chair beside each. Three wooden wardrobes stood against the opposite wall, and in between were pegs for jackets and caps. In one corner there was a stove. In the other a young man was pouring water from a pitcher into a basin. He was in his undershirt with a towel over his shoulder.

"Herr Braun," Kurt addressed him with deference, "this is the new apprentice, Hans Haupt."

Hans set down his satchel and stood at attention. Again he felt himself pinned and examined like a butterfly on a drawing board.

The man's voice was crisp but kind. "Good evening, Hans. Kurt here is your senior in age and has had some previous training, and I myself am a Rider-Candidate. So now you, instead of Kurt, will polish my boots."

Hans's face lit up. He nodded happily. Nothing would be too little or too big.

Herr Braun pointed to the bed farthest from the washstand. "That will be yours," he said. "And the wardrobe opposite. Morning bell at five-thirty. Downstairs at six for stable duties. Then we have coffee and rolls up here before the morning lessons."

"We bring our own rolls," Kurt put in. "You have a bakery, don't you?"

"The best in Vienna," Hans said proudly, washing his brother-in-law out of his mind.

And so at last, after years of waiting, Hans's new life had begun. He found the discipline stern but the tasks simple. Wishfully he had pictured himself on a horse the very first day, with Colonel Podhajsky giving him individual instruction. Instead, he was put to tasks that would have made him blush at home—washing windows, polishing brass, sweeping the floor, dusting ledges and railings. And all of it he did with a fierce intensity, to be done with it.

But there were other tasks which satisfied him completely. On the first morning he was assigned three horses to water and feed and groom. His old friend, the stablemaster, explained this duty. "You will be responsible for three stallions," he said briskly, and he began naming the three. "Siglavy Brenta, Neapolitano Santuzza, and . . . " The man slowly let his eye travel over the stable, stall to stall.

Hans could scarcely breathe. Had the man forgotten that he, Hans Haupt, knew Borina well, had taken him to and from the opera for days, watched over him like a mother? And just when the anguish was more than he could bear, the man's face creased into a grin. "Your third charge will be . . . Maestoso Borina!"

"Oh, Herr Stallmeister, how can I . . ."

The man chuckled. "You can thank me by work! Polishing brass and boots, cleaning tack better than anybody, washing leg bandages. That's how! Now you may help feed."

Postponing the exquisite moment of facing Borina, Hans gave the other two horses their grain first. Then he went empty-handed to Borina's stall. He stood very still in a moment of panic. Would Borina remember him, accept him in his new role? Or would he be so eager for oats he would not care who fed him? Hans looked into the purple-brown eyes without saying a word. The stallion gazed back serenely. His nostrils opened wide, contracted, and opened again. He gave a low, rumbling whinny, then with infinite grace came over and nudged Hans's shoulder.

Hans was in paradise. From that instant his life took on a wholly new meaning. He took care of his charges zealously. When he dealt out their grain, he riffled it between his fingers, sifting out any dust or weed seeds. When he watered his horses, he made certain the water was fresh and cool. When he combed tails, he used his fingers as a comb, separating each long hair so none would be pulled out. When he saddled, he laid the pad carefully on the withers, then slid it back so that the body hairs were smoothed the right way.

The vast stable and the room above it were Hans's world. He was almost completely happy . . . except that each morning he saddled Borina and walked him across the Josefsplatz for someone else to ride. The man was Bereiter Wittek. Hans envied him, hated him, worshipped him. He could make Borina dance and leap and march as if it were the stallion's idea, not his own. It looked so easy, so effortless.

As the weeks passed, Hans began to chafe. A gnawing worry crept into his mind. When would he ever get to ride and learn the courbette? He had not had a single word with Colonel Podhajsky, had barely caught a glimpse of him. At night he thought of asking Kurt or Herr Braun, but always they were busy playing a never-ending game of chess, and Hans couldn't bring himself to put the question. So he kept on working and hiding his worry deep inside.

## 19. THE FOUR-LEGGED PROFESSOR

HANS had almost despaired of ever speaking to Colonel Podhajsky again when the stablemaster tapped him on the shoulder one early morning. "Quickly go and wash. Put on a clean uniform. Herr Hofrat is summoning all the apprentices to the Riding Hall. Sharp at seven!"

Hans and Kurt almost collided running upstairs. They dressed in a fever. While Hans polished shoes for both, Kurt sewed missing buttons and a ripped seam. They took turns washing and combing before the tiny mirror, then went rattling down the steps as if the building were afire. Promptly they fell into line with the other apprentices. There were six in all. Being the oldest, Kurt led the procession. Hans brought up the rear.

Like foot soldiers they marched, step-in-step, across the street to the Riding Hall. Hans took a quick sidelong glance at the spot where he and Rosy used to watch daily for the Lipizzaners. She and Jacques were there now, first in the line of traffic, waiting for the stallions to go by. Without turning his head Hans waved to them by moving the fingers of one hand.

*Clop, clop. Clop, clop.* The boys' boots made clumping sounds on the cobbles. To Hans they echoed the pounding of his heart.

In single file the little company marched through the horses' entrance, through the anteroom where the horses were mounted, and into the Riding Hall. Just as the bells of St. Michael's were chiming seven, the austere figure of Colonel Podhajsky emerged from a side entrance. He strode

80

briskly to meet the boys and nodded formally as they lined up in front of him.

"Good morning!" he said, a smile softening his face.

"Good morning," six voices murmured in unison.

Again Hans was aware of the driving intensity of the man. He was aware too of a warmth that radiated through to him. He felt the dark eyes probing him, as if no one else were in the room, just the two of them.

"Young learners!" The Colonel's voice sounded deep and resonant, as if the earth spoke. "I hope some day to be addressing you as Rider-Candidates, and later as full-fledged Riding Masters. Meanwhile, your days of apprenticeship mark an epoch in your life. Here in the Spanische Reitschule," he said slowly, thoughtfully, "the great art of classical riding is brought to its highest perfection. This art is a two-thousand-year-old heritage which has come down to us from Greece, Spain, Italy, and of course France."

He spoke now with a kind of urgency. "Our Reitschule is a tiny candle in the big world. Our duty, our privilege is to keep it burning. Surely, if we can send out one beam of splendor, of glory, of elegance into this torn and troubled world . . . that would be worth a man's life, no?"

He stopped and waited in silence. No one said a word.

Hans nodded in solemn agreement.

"I congratulate you on your choice of a career," the Colonel went on. "But can you meet the challenge? How deep and passionate is your love for your profession, and toward the noble creatures entrusted to you?"

Again he stopped and waited, and again no one said a word.

"To learn this finest art," he resumed, "requires absolute mastery over body, heart, and mind. We test the young stallions for character and stamina. And we test apprentices for these same qualities."

He took a breath.

"This morning each of you will be assigned two professors. The first will be a Senior Riding Master who knows the strong and weak points of your horse and will be able to give you the right instruction at the right moment.

"The second . . ." he gazed intently from boy to boy " . . . will be a four-legged professor! The youngest apprentices will be given the oldest stallions to ride."

Hans's heart turned a somersault. That would mean Borina for him!

"Let me warn you, however, that your four-footed professor takes his role very seriously and his teaching methods are not always a joy to his pupils."

He paused. "It is a nice coincidence that there are six of you and that we have six teacher-stallions, each a member of a different dynasty." He began telling them off on his fingers: "Pluto, Conversano, Neapolitano, Favory, Siglavy, and Maestoso."

The names crackled in the stillness of the hall. It was strange how the mere mention of one name could make Hans tremble. His mind raced ahead. He saw in a flash Borina teaching *him* the courbette. How quickly he would learn . . . in one or two lessons! He saw himself in the saddle, erect as a carven image, giving the signals with such skill that Borina again became the champion courbetteur of the world.

The Colonel interrupted Hans's vision. "There was once a wise horsemaster, Antoine de Pluvinel, whose holiest commandment was, 'Be miserly with punishment, generous with rewards.'

"But I am getting ahead of myself. What all of you want to know, what *everyone* wants to know, is the mysterious language between horse and rider; namely, what signals are given to inspire the stallions to perform their wonderful feats above the ground."

An audible sigh traveled down the line as six young men waited, all senses alert.

"Ach, my children, those aids," the Colonel said almost mischievously, "must remain a mystery. For now. You see, in many ways you are like the Lipizzaners. Their training takes, on an average, five years. Yours will take no less."

Five years! *Five years!* Hans felt the heavy finality of the words. They were like a physical weight on his head, his shoulders.

On the way back to the stables they rang in his ears, like a bell that will not stop tolling. "That's so long," he cried inside. "Why, it's forever."

# 20. THE FIRST MILESTONE

IMMEDIATELY after the lecture Hans was assigned his two professors. Maestoso Borina he trusted and loved, and the stallion returned that trust in full. The mystery of what he knew and what Hans did not know was to be shared at last. Like magic, the weight of the five years lifted.

Proudly Hans stood in the deep sawdust of the Riding Hall alongside his snow-white professor. He was in a state of high excitement over their first lesson together, never doubting that in a month, or two at most, he and Borina would be courbetting across the arena to the complete amazement of Colonel Podhajsky.

Hans's two-legged professor was Bereiter Wittek. The man had a sharply chiseled face, like a face on a coin, and he had the bluest eyes Hans had ever seen. Hans soon learned to regard them as a barometer. If they were mild blue, like a cloudless sky, all was well. But if they froze ice-blue, then Hans knew something had gone wrong.

Within the hour the riding arena became a whirl of merry-go-rounds. White horses on white lunge-lines were trotting around and around in a circle, each horse held on a guide rein by a Riding Master, each one mounted by a young apprentice without reins or stirrups.

The longed-for moment had come at last. Hans was riding Borina! But it was not like the dream. It was a shock, a defeat. Without reins he felt awkward and insecure as a baby. What was the matter? As a five-year-old

83

he had ridden a Haflinger bareback. Could reins make that much difference? He was tossed and bounced on the saddle like a ship on a rough sea. Borina seemed to be going a hundred kilometers an hour, and at any moment might buck. In desperation Hans tried cramping himself with knees and legs to keep from kiting into the air. Even so, the slap of his seat on the saddle resounded like the slap of waves on the hull of a ship.

His muscles balked at the cramped position. He grabbed onto the pommel of his saddle, clinging for dear life.

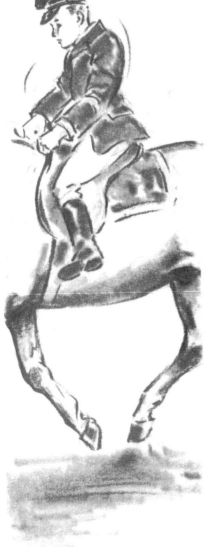

Directions came spitting at him like flak:

"Sit *in* the saddle, not *on* it!"

"Sit on your two seat bones."

"Push the horse ahead with your seat."

Hans blanched. He did not want to push Borina ahead; he was going fast enough! He longed to pull him down to a walk, but he had no reins!

The jolting trot went on, and the pelter of commands:

"Head up! Don't pull it in like a turtle."

"Your legs dangle like spaghetti. Keep them steady."

"Heels down!"

"Shoulders back!"

"Hips forward! Don't collapse at the waist!"

"Eyes ahead!"

And just when Hans felt that his spine might snap in two, Bereiter Wittek reeled in the lunge-line, slowing Borina to a walk.

The man was patience itself. "Ach, Hans," he pleaded, "riding a Lipizzaner is like music. Music has rhythm, a beat. You must adapt your rhythm to that of Borina's. You should enjoy it, like flying on a magic carpet. What must he think, Hans, when your arms and legs flap like a bird? Now then, try again, try to be with Borina through your seat bones."

And so Hans's first lesson was a rude awakening. How much there was to learn! But his devotion to his purpose never flagged. The difficulties only made him more determined.

At the end of six months Hans was still riding without reins, without stirrups.

"Do not think stirrups," Bereiter Wittek cautioned. "Do not admit them into your mind, ever."

Hans obeyed to the letter. He did not even look at pictures where riders sat snug and secure, their hands steady on the reins, their feet in the stirrups. Was not the courbette ridden without stirrups? For the goal ahead he could endure the slow and painful months of learning.

His progress was as changeable as the weather. Sometimes he seemed to forget everything, even such elementary rules as focusing straight ahead, eyes on a line between Borina's ears. At other times he did everything right.

One day he and Borina seemed especially attuned. They were cantering around and around in lilting rhythm, the same number of paces each lap. Hans felt himself immortal, like some Greek god flying along the plains of Olympia. The breeze—of Borina's own making—washed his face, and the cadenced rhythm carried him so effortlessly he wondered if people ever died of sheer happiness. "What does it matter," he asked himself, "that Bereiter Wittek holds the guide reins? What does it matter if *he* paces Borina? It is Borina I ride! Borina skimming me around and around, and up, down, up, down, on coiled springs. Oh, Mamma," he sighed, "it wonders me if I am in a dream."

"*Gut! Sehr gut!*" the Bereiter beamed. "I like it how you sit firm yet relaxed. Your spine is now a fine shock absorber."

The rewarding words were so unexpected that Hans went tense. His arms, legs, back grew rigid as rods.

Herr Wittek halted Borina in mid-stride. His eyes darkened with sudden intensity. "Alas!" he sighed heavily. "We must now go back to first lessons. Make windmills of your arms, Hans. And whistle to relax more."

Red-faced, Hans rotated his arms and began to whistle, and the tune he chose burst out of him without thinking. It was the song of Ramerrez, and he whistled with all the passion of the outlaw, "Oh, let her believe I have fled to freedom."

The stallion's ears pricked sharply. Hans could feel the hindquarters ready to crouch. For a wild instant he hoped Borina would spring into the air . . . ten times!

"Whoa! Whoa!" Bereiter Wittek stilled the impulse at once.

Sedately Borina fell back into a walk, head low. But his ears were still lively, as if to say, "We almost played a joke on the Bereiter, eh, boy?"

The days slid one into another while Hans grew in wisdom and in suppleness. He learned to let gravity pull him deep down into the center of the saddle, and to let gravity take care of his legs too, so that while they were hinged loosely to his body, they hung straight down just behind the girth strap. Meanwhile, his hands lay motionless and relaxed on his thighs.

Nights meant work, too. He and Kurt did suppling exercises in their room. Under the friendly direction of Herr Braun, they straddled chairs and kicked their legs out sideways to lengthen their inner thigh muscles.

"This is important," he explained to the boys. "Lipizzaners, you see, are bigger-barreled than other horses; so you must stretch your muscles to compensate."

They exercised wrists and fingers, flexing them as if they were a Mozart playing scales. And to develop control of their back muscles they lay flat on the stone floor, bent their knees and raised their seats while their shoulders remained firmly fixed on the floor. After thirty minutes of competing with each other, the boys fell laughing and exhausted into bed and slept soundly until morning bell.

With all the rigorous training, still it was many months before Hans could sit the walk, trot, and canter to satisfy Bereiter Wittek. All this time he was passenger only. When finally he was allowed to take the reins, he had almost forgotten how to hold them! Bereiter Wittek had to position his hands, evenly and together.

"Even hands mean even pressure on both reins," he explained. "Now then, is Borina well up on the bit?"

Hans nodded in ecstasy. For the first time he knew what this meant. It was almost as if his hands were the warm, living bit, and there was no cold steel in Borina's mouth at all. He and Borina were in contact! He shifted forward in his saddle ever so slightly. The response was instantan-

eous. On a straight line Borina started to walk. Hans counted the strides like the beats of marching music: *One-two . . . one-two . . . one-two . . .* They were uniform in length. They were regular as a metronome. Hans wanted to shout for joy. Riding Borina was like thought transference! It was like blowing a whisper into the air and turning on stars. At last, at last, he had passed the first milestone.

To celebrate, Hans rushed home after stablework was done. It was warm for March. The sun swam across the sky, melting the last patches of snow, and crocuses in the parks were a medley of color.

"Let's all go for a picnic!" he cried as he burst into the kitchen. "I'm riding with reins now!"

Jacques made a flying tackle and kissed Hans boisterously, first on one cheek, then the other. "I'm ready!" he shouted. "I want to go to the Prater and ride the roller coaster and the giant wheel in the sky."

"But the cost . . ." Mamma and Anna exclaimed in the same breath. "And who is doing your work at the Reitschule?" Mamma added.

"Kurt is feeding for me." Laughing, Hans spilled two silver schilling and a handful of groschen out of his pocket onto the kitchen table. "See? I am rich!"

Henri hooted. "Let the grand cavalier pay! High time he learned ze value of money." And he slapped his thigh to punctuate his remark.

Mamma began slicing ham and getting out the sweet-sour pickles. She sent Hans and Jacques off to the amusement park by themselves with a bulging box of lunch. There they bought pink soda pop and ate at once so they would have nothing to carry. Then they not only rode the roller coaster and the giant wheel, but they tried their skill at the shooting gallery, and paddled a rowboat on a little lake. Afterward, Hans taught Jacques how to exercise for suppleness and strength the way he and Kurt did every evening.

As twilight fell they returned home, tired and content. Hans's mother was busy at the stove, and when she was not looking Hans slipped one schilling and the remaining groschen into her apron pocket.

The supper was his favorite—wiener schnitzel, and for dessert thin pancakes stuffed with strawberry jam. Then in the chill of evening he went whistling back to his room above the stable and slept the sleep of the happy.

# 21. BORINA PLAYS A TRICK

AS THE months of training went on, Hans returned home less and less often. He could not bear to hear Henri's familiar taunt: "Well . . . boy? When you going to get off ze ground?" The question stung. The more so because Hans himself wondered, and he had no answer.

His whole world now was the Hofburg—the stables on one side of the Josefsplatz, the Reitschule on the other. Lessons and work intensified. A string of young, iron-gray stallions arrived from Piber. Stable duties doubled. Added to his own work on the more advanced gaits, this left little time for observing the Senior Riding Masters at practice from ten until noon each day. How was he ever going to learn the mysteries of the courbette if he couldn't watch how it was done? He envied the visitors who dropped in on daily rehearsals. He would gladly have given half his wages for the privilege.

Everything was different on Sunday. Then Hans tiptoed up to a corner of the gallery and watched Borina ridden by Herr Wittek during the regular public performance. Hungrily he studied their courbette. It was always magnificent perfection, full of animation and joy. But it puzzled Hans that both man and stallion seemed content with two leaps. As he watched, a dream grew in him, a resolve to inspire Borina to lift that thousand pounds again and again, to make him a champion once more. The ambition deepened as the weeks went by, but Hans was still working on the ground with no promise of when aerial work would begin.

On the anniversary of their second year, Colonel Podhajsky addressed the apprentices as they stood in a line underneath the Imperial Box.

"Congratulations," he greeted them warmly, "on surviving your rigorous early training! Thus far only one of your fellow-apprentices is missing." His face grew serious. "I urge all of you to believe that it is no disgrace to be dismissed. I can think of no other art—painting, sculpture, music, poetry— that demands more iron self-discipline than the life here. If you should be told you have not the stamina nor the talent to continue, be comforted by the knowledge that there are many less exacting professions."

Hans was aghast. Failure had never occurred to him.

"How soon you are ready for work *über der Erde,*" the Colonel was explaining, "depends upon individual progress. Another year for some of you. Even longer for others."

The silence that followed on his words was awesome.

"Come, come," the Colonel smiled. "The time will fly like that!" And he snapped his fingers to show how fast it would go. "To develop a good seat—pliant, upright, deep—is a subtle and difficult art. Unless your balance is perfect, you will disturb the balance of your horse. In short, you must achieve a perfect unison on the ground before you are ready to fly."

He started to say more, but there was a shuffling of feet overhead as the balconies began filling with the ten o'clock visitors. At the same moment a stableboy entered the hall, leading a bright bay Lipizzaner. He handed over the reins to Colonel Podhajsky.

The Colonel eyed the dark fellow in affection. Then with obvious eagerness to get into the saddle, he mounted in one easy motion and rode off. To Hans's joy he could recognize the "collected walk," the horse's head almost vertical, the hind legs well under the body, the action elevated.

Almost as if the Colonel's words had been a warning, a second apprentice was dropped the following week. This did not make Hans work harder, for he was already working the sun up and down. Some nights before undressing he fell onto his bed intending to read a technical book of instruction. But he was so tired that after a page or two he fell asleep in the glare of the light bulb. And if Kurt did not waken him, he slept through the night, with his clothes on. Yet with all his work he was happy, like a journeyman who knows he is on the right road, with the right horse under him.

In the beginning Borina had readily accepted Hans as a green pupil and had taken him through the elementary paces with little guidance. But as time went on, Hans began to see that it was not Bereiter Wittek who was the stern taskmaster. It was Borina!

One morning in full view of Colonel Podhajsky he gave Hans a sharp lesson. Bereiter Wittek had asked for the *passage,* or Spanish Step, which Hans already knew as a swinging trot with high action. He had ridden it several times, and always he had the heady sensation of scudding on a cloud, so high and suspended were Borina's steps.

Always before, Borina had performed the passage with measured cadence. Yet today Hans sensed a change in him. Was it skittishness? Boredom? Hans couldn't help asking himself, "Will I give the aids strong enough; or too strong so that he might break into an extended trot?" Carefully he positioned his hands, reassuring himself, "Why, Borina collects easily. Already he gives the forward impulse. Now! Drive him forward with your legs! Hold him back with your hands! Keep his head almost vertical!"

Hans's spirits soared. He felt himself into the trot, thought himself in full control. Borina was stepping forward with great liveliness. But Hans was blissfully unaware that the stallion was playing a trick on him. He was indeed stepping forward with high front action, but he was not following up with his hindquarters; he was shuffling along, swinging his hind legs in a lazy, dragging motion.

Nothing escaped Colonel Podhajsky. He was fascinated by the cunning of Borina. Bereiter Wittek too was struck dumb.

The silence grew as the false trot went on. The only sound was made by Borina, a kind of snort with each stride.

"What a swindle Borina pulls!" the Colonel chuckled as he rode alongside Herr Wittek. "The teacher-horse gives an unforgettable lesson, eh? It's clever how he decides to be lazy when the aids come too little and too late!"

Hans never knew how he managed to finish the lesson. It was horrible, this failure in front of the Colonel.

That night his dreams were dark and mysterious. He was in the Riding Hall, and Borina was the only living thing in the dark, and his feet had four toes like prehistoric horses—only they were long, like fingers, and very white. With those creepy front toes he was pointing around to his hocks, and his snorting laughter was so real that Hans awoke drenched in sweat.

All the rest of the night he lay worrying, wondering if Borina would ever have confidence in him again; wondering if he would be the next apprentice to be sent home.

## 22. BETWEEN THE PILLARS

TO HANS'S great joy and relief, he was not sent home.

Instead, everyone seemed kinder to him. Bereiter Wittek's "Good mornings" had a warmer ring. Kurt offered to teach him how to play chess. The stablemaster paid him a rare compliment. "Hans," he said, "you give your horses prideful care. I like that."

Even Borina seemed more affectionate. Under his mask of dignity, a lurking gaiety expressed itself in playful nudges and loud whinnies of recognition.

And so the blunder was soon forgotten, and the training went on. For Hans the next year was filled with anguish and ecstasy. He had reached the crucial point in his career. He must solve the mystery of the courbette, or he might as well be condemned to a lifetime of drudgery in the bakery. His one idea was to merge his identity so completely with Borina's that when he himself graduated to aerial movements, he could *will* Borina to leap more than two times. One or two leaps seemed like a withholding of his power. Hans remembered the Colonel's words: "Borina pulls a swindle, eh?" Was it possible that Borina was swindling Bereiter Wittek each Sunday? Sometime he would find out.

Meanwhile, there were days when Hans didn't know whether he was making progress or not. In the quiet sunlit hall Bereiter Wittek would bark his commands:

"Tempo one!"

"Tempo two!"

"Tempo three!"

Hans obeyed, carrying on his inward dialog, interpreting swiftly for himself. Tempo one at the canter: change lead every stride. Tempo two: change lead every second stride. Tempo three, every third.

"Left lead!"

With trigger control Hans brought back the calf of his right leg, but just a fraction. He flexed Borina's head left, but only a hairbreadth. He shifted his weight onto his right seat bone. He brought back his left shoulder. In perfect union he and Borina executed the flying change of lead at the canter. With every lesson Hans tried to refine his signals until communication became so secret that only Borina was the wiser.

Week by week the work stepped up in pace. Alone, and in groups. With music, without music. From the walk, trot, canter he graduated to the intricacies of the pirouette. Borina played no tricks here; he threw himself into the movement with such gaiety and precision that Hans couldn't help catching the rhythm. Pivoting on his haunches, forelegs stepping high, Borina danced around his hind feet as if they were nailed to one spot. In a flash of remembering Hans saw the porcelain statues in the shop windows next to the tobacconist. He and Borina were molded together . . . just like that. Except he and Borina were *alive!* Waltzing!

The days flowed together. The pirouette and the passage became habit. Muscles were doing the memory work. By daily repetition they acted intuitively, faster than thought. Less and less Hans carried on his dialog with his inner self. Yet the more proficient he became, the more impatient he was to go on. He had come to the Riding School to learn the mighty leaps above the ground.

Every night he studied them in the book of instruction which Fräulein Morgen had loaned him for the tenth time. There was no falling asleep now; he was too near his goal. He studied the pen-and-ink drawings of the aerial maneuvers. Just by blinking Hans could bring them alive! In color! Then he closed the book and did the courbette in his mind. He was glad that this was Borina's specialty. The capriole with its movement of horizontal flight was spectacular, breathtaking; the horse appeared to do the splits in midair. But to a horseman like himself, the courbette was greater.

Any powerfully built stallion who could do a succession of forward jumps, holding himself erect on his hind legs, and carrying a rider besides—well, that was. . . . He sighed deeply, unable to think of a word big enough.

One night when Herr Braun was putting the chessmen back into their box, Hans dropped his book, walked over and confronted him. "Sir!" he asked in exasperation. "When will I ever begin the airs above the ground?"

The Rider-Candidate showed surprise. "The work you are doing on the ground," he said, "is perhaps more difficult than the work above the ground. One leads to the other—but slowly. If you are so impatient," he added almost brusquely, "you should return to your bakery."

Hans stood as though someone had struck him hard across the face. His mouth opened, but no sound came out. Becoming a full-fledged Riding Master was the only way he could see how he could live. Like a puppy who had been booted, he went over to his end of the room. In silence he put his book away in his wardrobe. In silence he undressed and crawled between the covers. He stared fixedly at an invisible spot on the ceiling. For a moment he blamed the naked electric light bulb for the moisture in his eyes. He knuckled a tear away.

"Ach, Hans," the voice of Herr Braun was more gentle now, "all good growth is slow growth. Like a tree. You still have much work ahead on the piaffe between the pillars." He spoke slowly, emphasizing each word. "You see, Hans, the piaffe is the first stage for all aerial work. It is like a base from which the rocket flies! Only a horse and rider who do it well can work together above the ground."

"Thank you, sir," Hans sighed, resigned to the truth. Always there seemed another year, another month, another movement, another step, another something before he got his chance.

The very next day Bereiter Wittek ordered Borina readied for the piaffe, wearing the padded noseband with rings attached. Had Herr Braun confided last evening's conversation? Hans was too breathless to care, almost afraid to believe he was getting so near his goal.

"At last, Hans, we try you on the piaffe," the Bereiter said. There was a hint of pleasure in his voice as he tied Borina between the posts. "This for you is a big step forward. Now then, Hans, do you know what the piaffe is?"

"Yes, sir. It is a prancing in place, with very short steps. It is a sort of . . . " Hans hesitated.

"Of what?"

"A sort of . . ." Hans was afraid to put it into words.

Herr Wittek clapped his hands in impatience.

" . . . a getting ready for the courbette," Hans blurted out.

"Exactly! Now let's see if you can do it."

At first, sitting there proudly on Borina's back, Hans's heart flooded with energy, with the promise of the future. Borina lifted his legs like pistons and put them down again in the selfsame spot. Through every fiber of his being Hans could feel the lofty upward thrust. Up and up, never advancing, never backing.

Then, startled, Hans suddenly felt a strange lateral movement. He was bewildered. "Something's wrong," he told Bereiter Wittek.

Quickly the man untied Borina. "Trot him away. Very extended. Then come back to me."

Hans did as he was told.

"Always after the piaffe," the Bereiter explained, "a stallion must have a relief from the muscle tension of the short, sustained steps."

"Yes, sir; I understand, sir. But what happened? I felt a change in Borina's action. He suddenly seemed to go sideways instead of up. What happened?"

The Riding Master's head nodded. He was smiling, like a father whose boy has earned his first merit badge. "Borina ignored your signals at the beginning," he said. "He did the piaffe without any real guidance. Then, he expected some help from you. You must have been giving strong aid on one side and weak on the other. Now, see if you can give even pressure with both legs."

After the third try, followed by the free-moving trot, Herr Wittek ordered Hans to dismount and reward Borina. "I must reward you, too, Hans. You quickly sensed the ugly lateral movement and corrected your error. To me this shows promise for your future."

Hans was too happy to reply.

Glowing with pride, he took the small leather pouch from his pocket and poured a mound of sugar onto the palm of his hand. Borina lipped it in slobberly fashion. As he ground and swallowed the juicy sweetness, he eyed Hans familiarly, as much as to say, "It's been quite a session, eh, boy?"

## 23. A RASCAL IN THE GALLERY

THE following Saturday, like a flash of lightning Colonel Podhajsky announced the news, looking directly at Hans: "One of our Riding Masters is taken seriously ill. Bereiter Wittek will ride his stallion in Sunday's performance, and we'll need you, Hans, to ride Borina."

"Me?" Hans asked with a quick catch of his breath. He looked into the dark eyes questioningly. Why, this was like skipping a year in school, almost like graduation!

The eyes smiled back. "You will take part in the last event only, the quadrille. Now then, at ten o'clock this morning we rehearse—to music. There will be the usual tourists and visitors in the galleries; so it will be like a regular performance. Be saddled and ready for your entrance at eleven."

Hans was terrified and thrilled all at the same time. He had never worked before an audience. The galleries had always been empty. Besides, the quadrille was the grand climax of the entire ballet. Next to the aerial leaps, he thought it the most beautiful of all. For a year now he and the other young riders had been practicing the precise figures—the turns and movements on two tracks, the flying change of leg on the canter, half pirouettes, full pirouettes, the passage and, last of all, the piaffe. He knew them! He was ready!

He put on the cinnamon-brown frock coat and the bicorn hat belonging to some previous rider. "You'll have your own someday," the tailor

95

told him. "That is," he added, clapping Hans on the back, "if you have better luck than the last fellow who wore this."

Eleven o'clock came. In the anteroom of the hall the eight riders silently mounted their snow-white stallions, and silently lined up. Then to the airy music of the Polonaise they entered the great hall as at a performance. Colonel Podhajsky led the procession, followed by Bereiter Wittek, then Hans on Borina, then Herr Braun. Hans felt tremulous yet somehow secure between these two men who wanted him to succeed. Borina was serenity itself, his ears busy with the music, pulling in the familiar melody.

The music heightened the pleasure for Hans, too, as they paraded in stately fashion between the red-white-and-red flags that crowned the training pillars. Keeping his body erect, his shoulders parallel to Borina's, he felt in perfect harmony, felt himself ready for tomorrow's performance! Ready for anything! Even in the entrance-walk, the joy of rhythm, the pride in Borina filled him with such a fullness that he wondered if the buttons on his uniform might spew into the air. Of all the stallions Borina seemed most buoyant, most obedient.

Up in the galleries the morning visitors were on hand. Hans had been carefully schooled to be oblivious of them. He tried to remember this as he sensed a movement in the first gallery. He was turning in a platoon of four when his attention was caught by a blue beret waving wildly. Out of the tail of his eye he saw the figure of Jacques leaning far out over the railing. And sitting behind him, the boy's father, grinning.

In that hairbreadth of divided attention Hans unconsciously tightened his reins. Instantly Borina sank back on his haunches, raised up his body in the beginning of a courbette and dumped Hans onto the floor like a sack of potatoes. There was a soft thump as he hit.

The music did not stop. Nor did the complex pattern of the dance. Only Hans's heart stopped, then it bumped against his chest. He could feel the Colonel's glance like an icy finger. Overcome with misery Hans scrambled to his feet and caught up to Borina, who was setting one leg carefully across the other in cadenced movement with the other horses. Remounting, he closed the space which Herr Braun had kept open. Over and above the violins, he could hear guffaws and giggles from the galleries, and the sound of a slapped thigh.

Later, back in the stables, Hans worked in a trance. He took off the handsome coat that didn't belong to him anyway. He rubbed Borina dry

96

—under his saddle, along his chest, down his legs. The stallion submitted with pleasure, scratching his head against Hans's shoulder to relieve the itchy places where the bridle leathers had been. He still felt playful, and he nipped a piece of Hans's shirt without touching the flesh beneath.

In spite of his torn heart Hans neglected none of the routine. He took more pains, if anything, as if this were their last time together. "I don't blame you," he said, feeling the stallion's breath brushing against his cheek. "But what will I do now? How else can I live?" he asked, beseeching.

The limpid eyes held no answer. Only the boy's reflection in their purple-brown depths.

His grooming done, Hans closed the stall door behind him. He walked past the stablemaster, moved down the corridor, and up the worn stone steps to his room. It was empty. Carefully he hung his borrowed uniform in the wardrobe. He brushed the sawdust from the beautiful wine-brown serge and he buttoned up the silver buttons. Even third-hand, the uniform would still be almost as good as new. He put on an old shirt and a pair of work trousers, and pulled out his father's old brown satchel from under the bed. He packed in it the few clothes he had brought with him. They were too small now, but they would fit Jacques. As he snapped the lock, he heard a violent cough behind him and turned to see Kurt. With red-faced kindness the boy said, "Colonel Podhajsky is talking below with Bereiter Wittek. They want to see you."

"I know." Hans picked up his satchel. For a long while he stood in the doorway, glancing around the room in good-bye. He shook hands with Kurt. Then he squared his shoulders and went down the stairs.

The stable seemed deathly quiet. Herr Stallmeister, his assistant, the feed master, grooms, and stableboys all were going about their duties, silent and remote, like figures in a dream. Staring straight ahead, Hans took one heavy step forward, then another. He heard Colonel Podhajsky and Bereiter Wittek in low-voiced conference near Borina's stall. He moved toward them, toward what was going to happen to him. When he was within earshot, the talk ceased.

Time stood still. The Colonel's face was immobile. His hands were intertwined. Hans noticed their size and strength. They were clearly made to arouse a horse, to calm a horse, to lead a horse.

The man's eyes were fixed on the boy standing there, setting down the brown satchel as if it were full of stone.

"Hans Haupt! Whose fault was it?" The voice was an arrow.

Hans choked out the word. "Mine."

Again that probing gaze, that arrowlike voice. "You do not blame Borina?"

"Oh, no, sir. He was teaching me."

"And what about that rascal in the gallery? Was he to blame?"

"No, sir. He's no rascal; he's my nephew."

The Colonel paused. The merest wisp of a smile crossed his face. His attention seemed to wander down the aisle of stalls with the white faces and white ears listening. At last he said, "You have given the answer of a true horseman, Hans." He turned to Bereiter Wittek. "No art ever remains at the same level; rise and fall follow each other in eternal alternation. Eh, Wittek?"

The Riding Master nodded, and his eyes were the mildest blue.

Hans felt a floodtide of relief. He wanted to cry, to laugh. He wanted to do pushups, handsprings.

Before he could think what to say, Colonel Podhajsky laid a hand on his shoulder. "Here is one apprentice," he said, speaking to Bereiter Wittek, "whose eye will never stray again, no matter if forty elephants wave their trunks over the gallery." With that he made a grenadier turn and was gone.

Later that day a stableboy brought Hans a letter written on a square of lined school paper, In neatest penmanship the message read:

*Dear Uncle Hans,*
*I'm sorry I made you fall off. I did not laugh.*
*Your nevew,*
*Jacques*
*P. S. Rosy died today also. Mon père will now buy automobil.*

Hans read the letter twice. Then he re-folded it and tucked it away in his father's old satchel, in the pocket, very gently, as if it were a circlet of hairs from Rosy's tail.

It was like putting away the young years of his life.

## 24. I WILLED IT TO HAPPEN!

THE next day, during the Sunday performance, Hans went through the quadrille in complete command of himself and Borina. Watching only Colonel Podhajsky, as a musician watches the concertmaster, he cued Borina so skillfully that a regular spectator might not have noticed that a boy, instead of Bereiter Wittek, was the rider.

At the finale when he sat erect and immobile, doffing his hat in thanksgiving to Charles VI, Hans suddenly saw a vision of himself as a small boy in his nightshirt, praying in his little cubicle of a room: "Thank you, Lord, for my daily bread, and God bless Mamma and Papa and Anna . . ." And now in the few seconds while the musicians were thrumming their last flurry of notes, and while he held his hat at arm's length, he felt like that little boy again. His thanksgiving did not stop with Charles VI. It included Xenophon and Colonel Podhajsky and Guérinière and de Pluvinel and Papa and Prince Eugene and Bereiter Wittek and, most of all, Maestoso Borina.

It had been a long journey to this moment; yet even as Hans rode out of the hall to the pleasant sound of applause, his sense of triumph was tinged with a nagging worry. Time was slipping away. He'd be an old man before he did the courbette. Time was running out for Borina, too. If they didn't work together on this movement soon, how would he ever make Borina a champion again? He had to do it, he *must* do it, or else all of

99

his years at the Riding School would be like clawing and clambering up a steep mountain, without ever reaching the summit.

That noon, as he sat in the cafeteria with Kurt and the other apprentices, the food lumped in his throat and brought on an attack of hiccups. He alone of the four apprentices was still working on the ground. If only he hadn't fallen off when Borina reared; if only he hadn't looked up at the waving beret; if only Jacques had stayed at home!

A week later all of the *ifs* were washed away when Bereiter Wittek said quite calmly, "The time has come for your work above the ground."

The quiet words were a bombshell. Hans was standing in the center of the arena and it was very early in the morning, just past seven. Two other apprentices were working with their Riding Masters at either end of the hall. They seemed wholly unaware that today at this moment he, Hans Haupt, was about to learn the mysteries of the courbette. They were in a world of their own, unconscious of any other world. He too would be like that.

Bereiter Wittek read his thoughts. "Whatever happens now, Hans, no one will notice. To think you are being observed is self-conceit. The other riders and trainers are so busy sweating out their own problems that what happens to you is no matter; you could fall off a dozen times without their noticing. The truth is," he said, taking another notch in Borina's girth strap, "a fall or two is to be expected. I too have had my share."

He stopped as if his lecture were over, but it had only begun. "Remember, Hans, you must create a living work of art. The courbette must express sublime beauty. Instead of paintbrush and canvas, or chisel and stone, you work with living, responsive tools—muscle and sinew, and heart."

Hans nodded. He supposed there had to be all this preliminary talk, but he could hardly bear the delay.

The Bereiter now pointed to the special deerskin saddle. "Note there are no stirrups. Even in practice you will have no stirrups."

Hans nodded impatiently. He knew the courbette was ridden without stirrups. He knew that long ago from the pictures he'd pasted on his mirror, and from the time he had watched in rapture from the Imperial Box.

"So now you understand why, in the beginning, I wouldn't let you even think stirrups," the Bereiter was saying. "Balance is everything. Now I demonstrate!"

Hans felt as if every nerve in his body were quivering like the feelers of a butterfly. Straining to detect the aids, he watched the Riding Master mount Borina, ready him, walk him head on toward Hans. Suddenly Borina showed excitement. Nostrils distended, eyes fiery, muscles bulging, he knew what was expected of him. Then with pure animal grace he sank back on his haunches, lifted his body to a 45 degree angle, bearing his whole weight on his hindquarters. For the barest instant he seemed to freeze. Then he made a mighty leap forward on his hind legs before touching his forefeet to earth.

With all his looking, Hans had detected nothing—not a flicker of the Bereiter's hands, not a trace of movement of his legs.

In obvious pride Herr Wittek dismounted lightly as a boy, and rewarded Borina.

Now it was Hans's turn. And now came the spate of directions:

"Your hands—keep them quiet yet flexible.

"Your seat—steady and still.

"Your back—erect, slightly forward.

"Let your calves do the urging. But lightly.

"Restrain him with the reins.

"Time your hands and calves together. Promptly. Nimbly.

"Don't help too strongly!

"Don't hurry him!

"Don't pull up!"

His head spinning with do's and don'ts, Hans swung aboard. He collected Borina until he felt the stallion's readiness. Then trying to remember everything at once, he gave the urging aid with his legs, and in his eagerness to help, he lifted up with the reins so vigorously that Borina almost keeled over backward. And before Hans could blink, he was sitting deep in the sawdust. It was his second spill in a week!

Quick as a jack-in-a-box, he was on his feet, expecting the sharp criticism he knew he deserved. Instead, the Bereiter seemed to take the fall for granted. His voice was even and his smile kindly as he remarked, "That was a quick lesson, Hans."

Before the session was over, Hans tried once more. It was a near failure again. This time he leaned too far backward, and if the Riding Master had not barked, *Go with Borina!* Hans might have fallen off again.

Why was it so hard to think of the right things at the right time?

In the next few weeks Hans began to appreciate the subtleties of the courbette. He knew now why it had required so much preparation. It had

taken days just to understand what the Bereiter meant when he said, "Brace your back to form a supple connection with Borina's back." And it had taken many more days to do it!

Colonel Podhajsky studied Hans's progress with interest. As he stopped to exchange horses one morning, he rode over and spoke to Bereiter Wittek. "It is beautiful how he . . . " Hans waited for the rare compliment to himself, but the Colonel finished his sentence, " . . . how he sinks back on his haunches, hocks well bent, before he leaps. A superb test of balance!"

Then he turned to Hans. "I see that your balance improves, but it does not yet equal Borina's." His eyes twinkled. "Study the Prince Eugene monument, Hans. When you can sit like the Prince, then you are well on your way."

The proud morning came when Hans sensed strongly for the first time Borina's eagerness to leap. Quick as thought, Hans responded. He urged him with his legs, spoke to him with his hands. The signals and the readiness were timed. Then it happened . . . the beautiful perpendicular leap! At last Hans experienced the joy of flying.

"I just willed it to happen," he said shyly to Kurt and Herr Braun that night, "and it did."

Lessons went on. They were necessarily short because of the muscle strain on Borina. But each morning the miracle happened. And now Hans's resolve deepened. He tried to will a second courbette.

Bereiter Wittek suspected as much. "Ach, Hans," he said with warm understanding, "has it never occurred to you that Borina is nearing thirty, and slows down with age? Even he is mortal and destined to die."

"I don't think about it, sir," Hans replied. "I won't think about it!"

Bereiter Wittek's eyes shot sparks of blue. His voice was brusque. "If you can always influence Borina to do one magnificent jump, you will be a credit to the Reitschule and a surprise to me! Mind you," he waggled a sharp forefinger, "any stallion, *regardless of age,* that can leap even once on his hind legs is a great artist."

"Yes, sir," came the small, meek answer.

Hans had worked hard and long hours before. Now he worked harder, longer. He took up his old habit of evenings at the library. He studied Von Weyrother on the courbette. He studied Von Holbein. With Fräulein Morgen's help he struggled through the English works of the Duke of Newcastle.

By day he listened to Bereiter Wittek as if he were God handing down the Ten Commandments.

And yet, one mighty leap was all Borina would do for Hans.

"Maybe you should be satisfied with just one leap," Herr Braun suggested one evening as Hans was pacing up and down the room and around the everlasting chess game.

The pacing stopped suddenly. Hans wheeled about, not caring if the game was done or not. "I should quit now?" he demanded angrily. Then imploringly, "Please help me, sir."

"All right, all right."

The chess game was at an impasse. Herr Braun spoke in an aside to Kurt. "An intermission will do us both good." Then he turned to Hans. "You've got to *think* the second levitation," he said, leaning back in his chair, squinting through half-closed eyes. "You've got to think it before the first one is done. Think it right through your hands and legs and seat into Borina's being. Suppose you give yourself an examination. Write down precisely what you should do and when. Then tomorrow, do it! Sometimes it can be as simple as that."

Sitting on the bed, writing as fast as his pencil would go, Hans finished his list in less than ten minutes. After showing it to Herr Braun, he tucked it under his pillow. His sleep that night was dreamless, but even so the written words seemed to work magic. The next day Hans put them into action. To his utter joy Borina executed two spectacular leaps, one right after the other!

The aftermath was electrifying. When, next month, the programs were printed, Hans's name appeared twice. In the quadrille, of course, but where it mattered was in the seventh event: "Airs Above the Ground." There, in big black bold type was Borina's full name *Maestoso Borina,* and directly opposite, *Rider-Candidate Haupt.*

# 25. ONE BEAM OF SPLENDOR

NOW event followed event, like a string of popping firecrackers when you light the fuse. Kurt and Hans both were fitted for full-dress uniforms, bright scarlet with gold epaulets and yards of gold braid. And their heads were measured for new bicorn hats, in rich black with a golden cockade.

"But why?" Hans asked the tailor. "I thought the dress uniforms were worn just on special occasions. Like visiting royalty."

"Ja, I thought so too," Kurt chimed in, "or maybe some celebration out of history."

The tailor, a little penguin of a man with a tape measure tied about his middle, made a steeple of his flipper-like hands. "And what," he asked through a mouthful of pins, "could be more special than the visit of England's Prince of Wales? There's a man who has a good tailor!"

Kurt whistled in astonishment.

Hans's lips made an "O" but he couldn't get a sound to come out. To perform the courbette before royalty! If only his father could know.

He had little time to think in the few days before Sunday's gala performance. All hands were needed to polish every knob of brass, every marble crib, every square of window, every shiny plate of gold on every piece of tack. Morning lessons, of course, went on as usual, the discipline no more stern, no less.

Early in the week Hans made up his mind that his mother must see this special performance. Then in a burst of generosity he decided to include the whole family. In the end he dug deep into his earnings and bought six tickets. It was funny, he thought, how differently each person reacted to his gift. His mother cried into her apron. Anna hugged him. Jacques did a cartwheel right in the kitchen. Henri twisted his mustache; for once he was wordless and slapless. The policeman on the Josefsplatz clapped Hans on the shoulder. And Fräulein Morgen fortified him with a look that said, "I knew you could do it; and on Sunday you will."

When the day arrived, Hans, elegant in his new uniform, peeked into the empty Riding Hall to see if anything was different. He stopped short at the entrance, transfixed by what he saw. Swags of red-and-white bunting draped the lower gallery and were seemingly stabbed into place by great sheafs of live red roses. The reds were all alike; they even matched his own bright coat. He stood there a moment watching two men raking the sand and sawdust. It looked deep and soft. But when you were dumped off, it didn't feel soft. He flushed, remembering.

He sniffed the air in excitement. It was almost time for the visitors' door to open. He left the hall and went to the stable to see if Borina was ready. He looked over the stanchion and saw that he already wore the red velvet saddlepad trimmed with gold and the white deerskin saddle. An elderly groom stood by with bridle in hand. "How does it feel, Hans," he asked, "to be a Rider-Candidate and not have to do your own tacking any more?"

"I miss it," Hans confessed. "I like the way Borina reaches for the bit and clamps onto it as if he can't wait to get out and perform."

"Here then, you do it this morning. For luck."

Hans removed his white gloves. He took the gold-trimmed bridle, and standing at Borina's side he slipped the reins over the stallion's head, and offered the bit. Borina took it of his own accord.

"Ja, he *should* take it easy, like that," the groom nodded. "He's got experience."

The groom left. Borina and Hans stood eye to eye. They smelled the smells of each other. Borina blew the softest, whisperiest, hay-scented breath in Hans's face. Why don't people have such sweet breath, he wondered. He put on his gloves and rested his hands lightly on Borina's rump. Now came the interminable time of waiting, doing nothing. They sighed

105

in unison as they had done backstage at the opera.

All at once Hans straightened. Without really hearing it he was suddenly aware of music—solemn, festive, splendid—the entrance march. And he saw the Riding Hall in his head, not grand and empty, but grander, with the Prince of Wales looking young and elegant in the Imperial Box; and he saw both galleries full to bursting, and his own family in the left top gallery, level with the first chandelier; and Fräulein Morgen at the near end, facing the portrait of Charles VI. Hans placed them exactly in his mind as if they were chessmen. Then he would not be tempted to look up when his turn came.

So there was the whole audience, royalty and all, leaning over the red-velvet railing, eyes gazing fixedly on the first event. He thrust his hand in the inner pocket of his bright red coat and drew out the program. He knew it by heart but he read again.

The first number. Young Stallions. Six of them. He let his inward eye run over the youthful iron-gray fellows going through their paces—the collected trot, the extended trot, muscles rippling, hindquarters beginning to show power and propulsion. The picture in his mind stopped abruptly as four stallions were led past him on their way to the Riding Hall. They were next.

Excitement mounting, Hans suddenly couldn't endure the waiting. He moved away from Borina, stepped outside the stall, not wanting him to catch any part of his nervousness. He tried to wear blinders, but the whole glittering pageant seemed unwinding like a reel in his head. He saw the four middle-aged stallions doing all of the turns and paces of haute école. He saw even their tails fanning out in beautiful rhythm as they danced in circles and half-circles. He saw the *pas de trois,* the little drill of three with Colonel Podhajsky leading the maneuvers. He saw the horses step and pace and two-track, and he heard the applause and the music. And he lived through the work on the short hand-rein, and on the long, and he fancied he heard the gasp of the people, astonished that a man dare walk so close to a stallion's hindquarters.

And then at last he was in the anteroom to the arena—he and Kurt and Bereiter Wittek and the others, all mounted and ready. Now violins and cellos playing the *Wiener Blut* were sweeping them into the hall. And so they entered in the high feather step of the passage, the prelude to the "Airs Above the Ground."

It is the moment the audience has awaited. They clap their hands in anticipation. Borina's ears prick sharply. He is stimulated by the applause, beautified by it. Hans can feel the steady beating of Borina's heart between his knees. He can feel the airiness of his steps.

Hans is not aware of the audience. He is aware only that Time is racing away. The moment cannot last. He is riding in harmony with Borina, adapting himself to Borina's rhythm. The other stallions are performing their aerial routines, one by one, while he and Borina walk in quiet rhythm, awaiting their turn.

Bereiter Wittek now puts his horse into the marbled beauty of a levade. Ten seconds. Fifteen seconds. The applause bursts. When it dies he nods to Hans.

The time is now. The time for the courbette.

Hans guides Borina to the center of the arena. In a shaft of sunlight, more dazzling than spotlight, everything suddenly dissolves into unreality. The hum of excitement is voiceless, expectant, as Borina crouches on his hindquarters until, prompted by Hans's invisible cue, he rears up with one graceful fluid motion. The audience holds its thunder as Borina galvanizes his muscles, then leaps forward. At the moment his hind legs return to earth, Hans helps him spring up and forward once again. Hans barely breathes. It is Borina whose breath is heard as he leaps a third time! A fourth! And yet a fifth! It is Borina whose animal grace has reached the purest and most exalted heights of the courbette.

Like the roar of an earthquake the applause and bravos break loose. It is the moment of Hans's life. But he does not look up. He eases Borina into the Spanish Step and then down to the free walk. The moment is passing, is gone. It does not stand still.

When Hans went back into the hall to ride in the closing number, he felt a kind of sacredness in being part of the beauty of this ancient art of ballet. He understood with his whole heart and soul what Colonel Podhajsky had meant on that long-ago morning. "Our school is a small candle in a troubled world. If we can send out one beam of splendor, of glory, of elegance, it is worth a man's lifetime, no?"

In all of the turns and figures—the pirouettes, the flying change of leg at the canter, the lively cadenced trot, the shoulder-in movement—Hans thought, This is what joy is. Harmony between man and mount and music. He wished somehow he could be spectator and participant both.

Fräulein Morgen had anticipated the wish. She snapped a picture of Borina in the splash of sunlight at the full height of his courbette. Afterward she sent it to Hans, framed in red velvet. Underneath the picture she had written in her beautiful handwriting:

*He bounds from the earth
with the very exuberance of his spirits.*
*Xenophon.*

Hans examined the picture carefully, slowly. He studied the angle of the leap, the position of the haunches, the hocks, the bend of the forelegs, the arch of the neck. Then he looked at the rider. The face did not show. It might have been himself, or anyone he knew, or no one. The rider had somehow extinguished himself in order to glorify the horse, to make him look as if he had performed of his own will—joyously, gaily.

Now, at last, Hans understood the mystery.

# Epilogue

BORINA never recaptured his earlier record of ten courbettes, but he did achieve another distinction. He became the oldest performer in the history of the Spanish Court Riding School. In his thirtieth year he was still piaffing with vigor, and courbetting twice, and often three and four times in succession.

Then gradually his energy dwindled. But no one in the stable ever, for an instant, thought of putting him down. They coddled him with love. They ground his oats so he could gum instead of chew them. They added molasses for energy. And every day Hans took Borina for longer or shorter walks in the outdoor arena. The Viennese word for these walks is *spazieren*. It implies a leisureliness, a contentment, impossible of translation. But Hans and Borina needed no interpreter. They strolled side by side, neither one uttering a sound for minutes at a time, and then perhaps only a sigh of attunement.

After only a short period as a Rider-Candidate, Hans became a full-fledged Riding Master. He worked with the promising younger stallions now, teaching them to do, on command, what they had already been doing naturally. He had been trained by the finest professor, the great Maestoso Borina. Now he was passing on that learning.

Filled with the wisdoms of life, Borina died in the springtime of his thirty-third year. Meanwhile, far off in the Alpine meadows of Piber, pitch-black foals, full of the exuberant joy of life, were dancing and prancing. With no audience but their mothers, and no music except wind whispers, they were leaping into the air for the sheer fun of it.

And so the circle is complete. The great past and the future joined to perpetuate the Spanish Riding School of Vienna, the oldest of its kind in the world.

# About the Author and Artist

"Today's children and many adults believe that Marguerite Henry is probably the most successful writer of horse stories we have ever had," says May Hill Arbuthnot, noted authority on children's literature. "Her success rests on a sound basis. Every book represents meticulous research, the stories measure up to the highest standards of good storytelling, the animal heroes are true to their species, and the people in her books are as memorable as the animals."*

From the time she was ten years old, Marguerite Henry knew she wanted to become a writer. To date, she has written over forty books for boys and girls, most of them dealing with horses or dogs. Many have received literary awards. Her KING OF THE WIND was awarded the Newbery Medal. MISTY OF CHINCOTEAGUE became a Newbery Honor Book and also received the Lewis Carroll Shelf Award and the Junior Book Award given by the Boys Clubs of America; JUSTIN MORGAN HAD A HORSE, also a Newbery Honor Book, was given the Friends of Literature Award. BRIGHTY OF THE GRAND CANYON won the William Allen White Award; BLACK GOLD, the Sequoyah Award; GAUDENZIA, the Clara Ingram Judson Award; and MUSTANG, the Western Heritage Award. MISTY and BRIGHTY have been made into theatrical movies; JUSTIN MORGAN HAD A HORSE and SAN DOMINGO, THE MEDICINE HAT STALLION (retitled PETER LUNDY AND THE MEDICINE HAT STALLION) are teleplays.

Mrs. Henry's books are almost always based on actual fact, and she takes extraordinary pains to make sure her facts are as accurate as possible. She enjoys working on location, whether it is Chincoteague Island, the Grand Canyon, Siena, or Vienna. When not traveling to gather material for her books, she makes her home in a horse-loving countryside in southern California.

Wesley Dennis, who worked so successfully as a "team" with Marguerite Henry, was a genuine down-Easterner—born in Massachusetts and brought up on Cape Cod. He studied art in both the United States and Paris, and after several years of free-lancing, decided that his real interest lay in country life, especially horses. In 1942 he wrote and illustrated his first juvenile book: *Flip*, the story of a flying horse. About the same time he began to illustrate a series of articles for hunting periodicals. Later he won acclaim as a highly successful and popular illustrator of juvenile books—especially vigorous out-of-door stories. He illustrated most of the Marguerite Henry books, in addition to many by other writers and several of his own. Until his death, in 1966, he lived near Warrenton, Virginia, where he carried on his painting and illustrating in the kind of surroundings he found most stimulating.

* *Children and Books*, by May Hill Arbuthnot. Scott, Foresman and Company.

Printed in U.S.A.